# The Day Sarah Ran Away

## THE SISTERHOOD PIE PACT

⇒ • ⇐

### BOOK ONE

## JANELL GOODRICH YORK

Scrivenings
PRESS
Quench your thirst for story.
www.ScriveningsPress.com

*Dedication—To my husband, Jimmy. You're my rock and my biggest fan. I couldn't do any of this without you. Thank you for loving me so well.*

*"When mothers talk about the depression of the empty nest, they're not mourning the passing of all those wet towels on the floor, or the music that numbs your teeth, or even the bottle of capless shampoo dribbling down the shower drain. They're upset because they've gone from supervisor of a child's life to a spectator. It's like being the vice president of the United States."*

*~ Erma Bombeck*

# PROLOGUE

"What messes us up most in life is the picture in our head of how
it's supposed to be."
~ Jeremy Binns

The grandfather clock in the hallway chimes twelve times. My husband's cell phone dings on the kitchen table. Dave must have forgotten to grab it after our argument.

I dry my hands on a dish towel and cross over to the table where his phone rests face up. Emma's picture fills the screen. Warning bells ring in my head. Why is she texting her dad so late? Is she okay? Has something happened? She needs me. Taking a few breaths to ramp down my habitual panic response, I click the passcode that opens his phone.

Dad, are you there?

My fingers tap over the phone's keyboard with rapid speed.

This is your mom. Your dad forgot his
phone. Is everything okay?

Three bubbles appear, then disappear. The moments waiting for her to respond have my imagination spinning images of Emma lying in a ditch somewhere.

After what seems an eternity but is probably less than a minute, she responds.

> Yes, everything is fine, Mom.

I can hear her scolding tone on the word *Mom*, knowing she thinks I'm being overprotective as always.

After a beat, another text comes through.

> I had a question for Dad. It can wait until he gets home from his trip.

The words sting, but I swallow them down. I text back a simple response.

> Okay.

While waiting for her to text a goodbye, good night, love you, anything, I notice a long thread of texts between her and Dave. A mental debate ensues as I stare at the screen. Several minutes pass, making it clear Emma's done with our conversation.

I should put the phone down and head to bed, but instead, I continue to grip the cell. I shouldn't read their conversation. It's wrong. My head nods in agreement, but flashes of past hurts—feeling like the odd one out when Emma and Dave are together—have my right index finger scrolling to the beginning of their conversation.

> Are you sure you have to tell your mom tonight?

> Yes, I'm sure.

I won't be home when you tell her. I
should be there.

I know, Dad, but I need to tell her
tonight.

She's going to be upset. You know that,
right?

Mom will be okay. It will all work out.
You'll see.

I don't know. You might just break her
heart.

# CHAPTER ONE

Eight hours earlier

T he rich aroma from the simmering homemade spaghetti sauce fills the kitchen. I dance in front of the stove to a song from an upbeat boy band playing on the radio—a musical group my daughter liked in high school. I sing along, "I am the boy of your dreams, girl," smiling as I stir the sauce. Dipping a spoon into the bubbly liquid, I lift it to my lips, careful not to burn my tongue. Tilting my head, I scan the assortment of spices on the counter. It needs something.

My phone dings. I rush to the counter to retrieve the device. Only a news notification. I sigh and set the phone down, only to pick it up again. Staring at the screensaver photo, I touch my finger to my daughter's smile. How long has it been since Emma texted me? How long since I saw her smile in person? I dial her number again, and my call goes straight to voicemail. How many messages have I left? A plop-plopping from the stovetop, followed by a loud sizzle, jerks me from my reverie. I grab my wooden spoon and give the sauce a quick stir, turn the burner to low, cover the saucepan, and wait.

Several dogs bark in our little cul-de-sac, which usually means the mail has arrived. Looking out our kitchen window, I see the white mail truck drive away. I head outside to check the box.

The new neighbor waves at me from her front porch, and I return the gesture. Judging by her bright-pink high-rise shorts and matching racerback tank, she's returning from a run. A few wisps of hair have escaped her high blonde ponytail. The loose tendrils frame her youthful face.

"Mrs. Goodwin, wait," she calls as I turn to go back inside.

I am not sure how she knows my name. Maybe read it on our mailbox? I stop and she jogs over to me, sweat glistening on her forehead.

"Hi. I'm Olivia Piercy." She extends her perfectly manicured hand. "I moved in a few weeks ago." She points to her house across the street.

"Nice to meet you. I'm Sarah." I return the smile.

After I shift the mail to my left hand, we shake. Olivia releases my hand and points to a boy and a girl riding bikes around our cul-de-sac. "Those are my kids. Mia is six, and Liam is eight."

Liam's short brown hair is damp from pedaling his bike. He sports a red muscle shirt paired with black shorts. Olivia motions for her kids to join us, but Liam continues to ride his bike in circles, popping a wheelie off the curb each go-around.

Mia races her bike to us, then stomps on the brakes. Her bike skids sideways, almost throwing her off its purple banana seat. Once she regains her balance, she looks up at me and smiles. With her deep-blue eyes and thick, long blonde ponytail, she is a carbon copy of her mother, except for her two missing front teeth. A mermaid graphic glitters on Mia's purple top.

Olivia wets her fingers with her tongue, bending down to rub dirt smudges from Mia's left cheek. The little girl giggles, then places her small tennis-shoe-clad feet on the pedals, setting the bike back in motion. Light flashes from her soles with each push.

Dave has been nagging me to clean out Emma's room. I wonder if Mia would like any of her *Little Mermaid* toys.

"Mommy, watch this." Mia attempts to pop a wheelie, but her tire barely leaves the pavement.

"Way to go, sweet pea." Olivia smiles and applauds.

The pride on Mia's face is reminiscent of toddlers I've seen throwing their hands in the air, thinking they are jumping high while their feet never leave the ground.

A large lump forms in the back of my throat as I watch the interaction between Olivia and Mia. "Enjoy them while you can," I say. "They grow up way too fast."

Olivia turns her attention back to me.

The threat of tears burns the backs of my eyes. I clear my throat. "My daughter is coming home today for a visit. Emma just finished her junior year of college. I've been cooking her favorite meal all day."

"Oh, how nice." Olivia smiles.

"Yes, I've missed her so much. It seems like only yesterday Emma was Mia's age, riding her bike while I watched from my porch." I gaze back at Mia while remembering a different little girl on a different bike. "Emma rode a neon-pink bike with silver flecks. She loved to clang the attached silver bell as she rode around our neighborhood. I'm sure the neighbors loved that." I laugh. "Her prized baby doll sat in a precarious position in the white wicker basket strapped on her handlebars." A wistful smile forms across my lips.

A loud beeping from the open kitchen door sounds. "Oh, no! My bread," I exclaim, panicking. "I have to go."

"Oh, okay." Olivia's voice drops, sounding disappointed. "Do you need help?"

"No, I've got it, but thank you for offering." I pat her shoulder, then whirl back toward our house. "It was nice to meet you, Olivia," I yell over my shoulder as I sprint up the sidewalk.

"Maybe we can visit longer next time?" she shouts behind me.

"That would be nice," I say before shutting the kitchen door.

Once inside, I notice a sweet yeasty scent now mixes with the tomato-herb aroma. Lowering the oven door, I'm met with a loaf of wonderful golden goodness. Perfect. I didn't burn it after all.

After slicing the bread and finishing the spaghetti noodles and sauce, I check the dining room. Crystal glasses sparkle under the chandelier. Porcelain china with delicate rosebuds adorn the table. Emma will inherit all the dinnerware handed down to me by my grandma once she's married. Exhaling a satisfied breath, I smile at my efforts.

I check my appearance in the large antique silver mirror hanging above the buffet sideboard. I'm wearing the emerald silk blouse Emma bought for my birthday last year over a pair of white capris. She said the blouse matched my eyes. My shoulder-length hair is straight and sleek. It took a lot of product and a straightener to tame my unruly auburn curls. Emma likes my hair better straight. She's blessed with her dad's thick, slick ebony hair.

"Wow, something smells delicious." Dave enters the living room. He stops in front of me. "You look nice." He places a tender kiss on my cheek.

"Thanks." I smile. "When did you get home? I didn't hear the garage door open."

"Just a few moments ago." He scans our living room. "Looks like you've been busy. What is all this?"

"Wedding stuff." I raise an eyebrow and fold my arms across my chest. "Remember? Emma's coming home for the summer, so we can start planning her wedding."

"I remember." His body stiffens. Dave frowns as his mocha-brown eyes travel from the wedding invitations on the coffee table, to the bridal magazines strewn on the couch, to the box of pictures on the floor. His gaze lands on my wedding dress draped over the brown leather recliner.

His eyebrows draw together, forming grooves on his forehead as he continues to stare at the dress.

My mind races. The frown on his face is the opposite of what I was expecting. Instead of asking why he looks so sour, I walk over to the dress and hold it up against my chest. "I know Emma is taller than me, but a skilled seamstress can add some lace to the bottom to lengthen the gown." Dave's silence makes me uncomfortable. "Of course, the sleeves will need updating. Thankfully, puffy sleeves are not in style anymore." I titter. "Maybe remove the lace around the neck." Flustered, I shrug. "I don't know what all it needs, but Emma and I will figure it out." Carefully spreading the dress back across the recliner, I continue, "Can't you see it, Dave? You walking Emma down the aisle in the same dress I wore at our wedding."

Misty-eyed, I raise my gaze from the satin-and-lace gown to Dave, who remains as motionless as a stone statue, frowning. What is wrong with him? Does he not want Emma to get married?

After a heavy sigh, he asks, "Have you talked to Emma recently?" He runs his right hand through his salt-and-pepper hair—a gesture he does when he's worried. "Is this what she wants?"

Confused by his question, I counter, "Why wouldn't she want this?" I wave my arms at the evidence displayed around us. "I want her to have her dream wedding."

Dave gives another long, low sigh. "Are you sure it's not the wedding of *your* dreams?"

My back bristles.

Biting my lower lip, I swallow hard. "This is our last summer with Emma before she graduates and begins her new life with Philip." A painful hollowness sinks deep into my stomach. Tears build, but I continue to defend my reasoning. "Planning this wedding will give me time with her before she becomes Mrs. Emma Polk. It's the last thing we get to do for her, Dave."

He rubs the back of his neck, and his posture sags. His six-foot-three frame seems to shrink before my eyes. "You should have talked to our daughter first."

I want to take his face in my hands and smooth the worry lines from his brow, but I resist. Frustrated, my body tenses. "Well, I would have if she would pick up her phone," I reply in a biting tone.

Dave releases an exasperated sigh, then checks his watch. "I don't have time to finish this conversation right now. There's a lot more that needs to be said, but it will have to wait."

"Oh, no, you don't. What more needs to be said?" I throw my arms in the air. "Whatever you are going to say, Dave, say it."

His face reddens. We stand toe to toe for what seems like an eternity. "We have a problem, Sarah." The words tumble out.

My throat constricts. The sinking feeling I had earlier hits the basement floor with a thud. My temples throb as I wait for him to explain. Images of Dave leaving me for a younger woman reel in my brain.

"Who is she?" I blurt.

"What?" His wild-eyed expression makes it clear an affair is not the problem.

My brain shifts with lightning speed, conjuring up another dreadful scenario. In a matter of seconds, I remember Dave saw his doctor yesterday for a checkup. With my brain in wedding overdrive, I forgot to ask how it went. "What did Dr. Jones tell you?" My voice is shrill, panicked.

"Sarah, calm down," Dave says. "You're letting your imagination run away with you again. I'm fine."

I take a deep breath in and exhale, willing my heartbeat to slow to a normal pulse.

"Then what is it?" I grow impatient.

A car horn blasts outside, and he swivels his head toward the front door. His taxi to the airport has arrived.

"You can't leave me hanging here," I plead.

When he turns back to face me, his olive skin pales so that the dark circles under his eyes are noticeable. My heart goes out to him, but I can't back down. I need him to finish what he started. "Please, Dave."

He glances around the room uneasily, then his intense gaze lands on my face. His eyes bore into mine. "Your obsession with Emma."

My mouth falls open and I take a step back. "You're ridiculous. Obsession?" Why has he been stressing me out for the past few minutes when I have more important things to attend to? "She's my daughter. I only want what's best for her." My chest heaves. "What kind of mother would I be if I didn't take care of her?"

His face reddens again. "She's not a little girl anymore." His scolding is loud, stern. "She's a grown woman. She has her own life now, Sarah."

"I know that." I match his volume and tone. "But I'm still her mother."

Dave throws his hands up. "Of course you are, but she doesn't need you like she did when she was little. You need to take your focus off her and find something new to get excited about. Every day, you mope around the house, waiting and hoping she'll call or come home. You need to make some friends, start a hobby, join a gym." Then he says, with slow precision, "Get a life."

My face stings from the imaginary blow across my cheek. I stand frozen. My gaze drops to the floor. I wish the thick carpet beneath me would become quicksand and swallow me up.

The taxi's horn blasts again.

"Do you have my overnight bag packed?" His voice is so quiet, I almost don't hear him.

Embarrassed and hurt, I point to the front door, keeping my eyes averted from him. His brown leather overnight bag sits in the corner of the entryway. He pivots to retrieve it, then throws it over his shoulder. "I have to go. I can't miss my flight. I hate to leave this way, Sarah."

I shrug, feigning indifference while mentally shrinking into myself.

He walks back to me and kisses my forehead. I keep my focus pinned to the second button of his shirt.

He exhales, then places his palm under my chin to lift my face until our eyes meet. "I love you."

Tears well in my eyes.

Dave's lips form a weak smile. "I hope you enjoy your time with Emma tonight." He releases me, pivots abruptly, then strides out the front door.

# CHAPTER TWO

"Get a life."

Dave's words replay on a continuous loop in my brain. What does that even mean?

I'm so mad at him for ruining my good mood. I take a few deep breaths. One, two, three, four, and exhale. Emma will be here soon. I need to be at my best.

Sitting on the living room floor, I pull the large plastic bin of family pictures onto my lap. Hundreds of photos of all sizes are stacked on top of each other. I regret never taking the time to put them in albums. Some of the photos show unfamiliar faces with no names written on the back—pictures inherited from my dad after he passed away.

Most of the photos are of Emma at different stages. Her first time walking, her first taste of baby food, learning to ride her bike, her kindergarten school picture. There are photos of Dave, Emma, and I posing in front of Cinderella Castle at Disney World, swimming in the ocean, and building sand castles on the beach. Emma's soccer photos start when she was four and continue every season until she graduated from high school. Nostalgia evokes an unspoken, wistful longing. Then a glimmer of hope flutters in my chest as I think of how many hours going through the stacks of photos with Emma will take. The thought of selecting the best pictures for the father-daughter dance video lifts my spirits.

*Get a life.*

"This is my life, Dave," I shout to the empty room filled with framed pictures of Emma's growing-up years.

An engine purrs in our driveway. My pulse quickens. Joy-filled adrenaline jolts me onto my feet so fast I drop the box of photos. Pictures scatter across the floor. Shaking my head, I throw my hands in the air. I'll deal with the mess later.

I run out the front door, reach her silver compact car, and wait for her to exit. Emma smiles. My heart melts as I wrap my arms around her in a big hug. The strawberry fragrance from her shampoo surrounds me.

After a long embrace, I release her and examine her from head to toe. Has she been taking care of herself? Eating right?

She blushes as she scans our neighborhood. "Can we go inside, Mom?"

"Of course. I have so much to tell you." My heart races. "I've made your favorite dinner, and there's dessert." I wink, then loop my arm with hers, mentally skipping down the sidewalk.

"I have a lot to tell you too."

Is it my imagination, or is she nervous? I frown, then dismiss the thought.

Once inside, Emma scans the living room much like Dave did earlier. She bites her lower lip as her warm brown eyes dart from one area of the room to the next.

Uneasy with her reaction to the wedding paraphernalia, I

try to ignore the anxious churning in my stomach. Dismissing the warning signs in my head, I grab the newly purchased wedding planner from the coffee table. "Look what I bought us. The lady at the wedding boutique store said it was a 'must have' to plan your wedding. Isn't this going to be so much fun?" I hold it out to her.

Emma stares at the planner but doesn't take it. Instead, her eyes slowly rise to my face. "We won't be needing that, Mom." She throws her left arm out toward me and wiggles her fingers. "Philip and I eloped last weekend."

My stomach drops. A blast of heat travels up my chest and neck, making me uncomfortably hot. I hear Emma's words, but comprehension eludes me. A knot lodges in my throat, so big I might choke on it. My mouth gapes open, but no words come out. All I can do is stand there staring, waiting for the room to quit spinning.

Once it does, I take her soft, youthful hand in mine to get a closer look. Her engagement diamond catches the light. It sparkles next to the newly acquired gold wedding band. My gaze travels from her ring to her face. Emma's big brown eyes stare at me, wide and unblinking as she presses her lips into a thin line.

"Congratulations," I say.

She releases a warm breath and lifts her lips into a half smile.

The excited adrenaline from a few moments ago has vanished. Tiredness overtakes me. I want to sit down, but my feet won't move.

"As you know, Mom, Philip graduated this spring."

Though numb, I nod for Emma to continue.

"Two weeks ago, he was offered a job in Phoenix, Arizona."

My chest tightens. Dread fills my heart.

Emma plasters on an enthusiastic smile and squeezes my hands tightly. "It's a really good job. He couldn't pass it up." She pauses. Then taking in a deep breath, she swallows hard.

My stomach lurches, knowing what she will say next but praying I'm wrong.

"We leave for Phoenix this weekend." Her words drop like a boulder. She stands staring, seemingly waiting for my reaction.

I flinch. My stomach lurches as the bottom falls out, and my happy expectations for the summer turn to dust.

My shallow breathing makes me lightheaded. My ears ring. I hope I don't pass out. My voice strains to ask, "What about college?" The words burn my throat. "You only have one more year to go. Couldn't you have waited another year?"

Emma releases my grip on her hand and takes a step back. Crossing her arms over her chest, she says, "Mom, I plan to finish, but that's for Philip and me to figure out." Color rises in her cheeks. She stands rigid and unyielding. "I know you had a lot of plans for us this summer, but the thought of living long distance from Philip for a whole year ..." Tears fill her eyes. "I couldn't do it."

"What about living long distance from me?" My chin trembles.

She drops her arms. "Can't you just be happy for us, Mom?" Her voice softens.

Taking her face in my hands, my lips quiver as I try to form a smile. "All I want is for you to be happy, but—"

The blare of the smoke alarm in the kitchen fills the house.

"Ugh." I huff. "Excuse me. I'll be right back." I spin and dash to the kitchen, leaving Emma standing in the middle of the pointless wedding mess.

I forgot I had set the stove burner on low to keep the marinara warm. What was once a colorful, flavorful red sauce is now a charred black lump stuck to the bottom of the pan.

My nose burns from holding back tears. This is not how I pictured today going. One tear escapes, trickling down my cheek, then another and another. Grabbing the dish towel nearby to dab at my eyes, I take a few deep breaths in and out —one, two, three, four—willing the tears to stop. Knowing I need to rejoin Emma, I swipe under my eyes one more time and return to the living room.

She sits cross-legged on the floor, a stack of photos on her lap. Her ebony hair is pulled up in her usual messy-bun style. Quiet, I stand in the entryway and watch her pick up one photo, then another, examining each one. A faint smile forms on her lips as she places them on the floor beside her.

Hot, heavy tears form behind my eyes again. I can't catch my breath. Two emotions war inside me—an overwhelming love for the girl sitting in our living room and the crushing disappointment that she's creating a life without me. An unexpected sniffle reveals my presence. Emma's eyes rise to meet mine. I plaster on a fake smile, hoping to hide how dismal I feel on the inside.

"I may have burned dinner." I blush, giving a hollow laugh.

Emma laughs too.

"How about pizza?" I suggest. A flood of memories cascades through my brain—us sitting around the kitchen table on Friday nights, sharing our day and laughing at silly things while stuffing our faces with pizza. A genuine smile replaces the fake one. We may not have all summer, but we can make the most of tonight.

Emma's gaze returns to the picture in her hand. Meekly, she says, "That sounds great, but ... Philip is meeting me at his parents' house. They want to take us out to dinner to celebrate."

My smile fades as I process what Emma said, letting her

words sink in. They knew before me. Nausea overtakes me at the realization.

The floodgates open. Tears stream down my cheeks.

Emma jumps to her feet and takes my hands in hers. "Mom, I know this isn't how you envisioned my wedding or this summer. Everything just happened so fast."

"It's not only the wedding. You're moving so far away." I cry harder.

"I know, but we can talk on the phone. You can come visit me when we're settled. I'll be home for the holidays. It will be like I never left." Doubt flickers in her eyes.

I nod. What more can I say?

"I love you, Mom, but I really have to go. Philip and his parents are waiting for me. I will call you later." Emma leads me by the hand like a child, out our front door, onto the sidewalk, and back to her car. She gives me a quick hug, then slides into her driver's seat, leaving me standing alone in the driveway. After backing out of our driveway into the circular part of our cul-de-sac, she rolls down her passenger window, leans her head out, and yells, "It will all work out." Then she looks straight ahead and drives away.

I stand in a stupor, staring until the glow of her taillights disappears.

I walk mechanically back into the house. My cell phone chimes in my pocket. Now what? Irritation replaces numbness. Begrudgingly, I pull it out to check the screen. *Michael Tiller.* Why is Dave's boss calling me? Has something happened? Is Dave okay?

"Hello?" My hand trembles as I answer.

"Sarah," Dave says.

"Are you okay?" I sputter, struggling to speak. "Why are you calling from your boss's phone? Did something happen?"

"No, no, everything's fine. I'm fine," he assures me. "I

forgot my phone at home. I wanted to let you know our plane landed. I didn't want you to worry."

"Oh, okay, that's good." I sigh in relief. There's a long pause between us. The thought of telling Dave about Emma's elopement fills my heart with dread. He will be so disappointed. He was looking forward to walking Emma down the aisle. With a mournful tone, I say, "Emma left."

Dave lets out a long sigh. "How are you doing?" Before I can answer, he adds, "I knew the news would be hard, but I wanted to check on you before my client meeting."

It takes me a moment for his words to sink into my overwhelmed, muddled brain. My body slumps onto the nearest kitchen chair. "Did you know too?" I pray I misunderstood what he meant.

"I did. But let me explain." His voice grows urgent. "Emma told me right before their elopement because Philip wanted my blessing."

I close my eyes and rub my temples. My head hurts from all the new information I'm processing.

"She made me promise not to tell you," he continues. "She knew you would try to talk her out of it."

I can't respond. The ringing in my ears is deafening.

"Sarah? Are you still there?"

"Yes, I'm here," I say flatly.

He sighs again. "I hate to do this to you, but my boss is holding the taxi for me. I'll be home tomorrow night. We can talk about this then." He pauses a moment. "Please don't be upset. Try to stay calm. I promise it will all work out." He repeats Emma's words back to me. "I love you," he says, and the phone clicks.

I sit quietly, crushed.

My head pounds more intensely now, threatening to burst. After a few minutes of holding my head in my hands, a rush of angry energy wells up inside me. Who will everything work out for?

I rise from my seat and grab a glass from the cupboard. Once I've filled it with water, I search for the Extra Strength Tylenol bottle. After throwing back two pills with a swig of water, I wrinkle my nose at the burned spaghetti-sauce aroma permeating the air. I eye the table. Two clean, empty plates wait to be filled.

Disappointment and betrayal prompt me to leave the kitchen. Before I go, I pull the trash can out of the pantry. I drag it across the tile, through the entryway, down the hall, and into the living room.

In one big sweep of my arms, the wedding invitation samples go into the trash can with a loud *thud*. The throbbing pressure at my temples builds, along with my momentum. A fresh burst of adrenaline drives me.

The wedding planner rests on the coffee table. Visions of writing in dates for cake tasting at Sunny's Bakery, choosing floral arrangements at Suzie's Blooming Flowers Shop, and selecting bridesmaids' dresses and groomsmen's tuxes at Bonnie's Wedding Imperium whirl in my thoughts like a dream. But reality crashes into my fantasy. Grabbing the planner, I step a few feet back from the trash can, aim, and throw it through the air. It hits with a loud *clunk* into the tall white plastic bin. "Two points, and the crowd goes wild!"

The pictures are strewn on the carpet in front of the couch. Averting my eyes from the faces in each photograph, I stack the photos in the tub and carry them back to the corner of the basement where I found them.

After straightening the living room, I grab the trash can and work on the kitchen. Along with the charred spaghetti sauce and dried-up noodles, the French bread has hardened, making it inedible. Our "special" dinner tops off the garbage can. Out of breath, I sit, overwhelmed with today's events. Soft music plays from the radio on the counter. I forgot to turn it off earlier. I listen as one song ends and another starts. A guitar begins playing a familiar melody. I recognize the song before the artist starts singing the lyrics to "Landslide" by Fleetwood Mac. My vision blurs. Needing to be anywhere but here, I grab my purse and sprint to my car.

# CHAPTER THREE

Not sure where to go, I drive up and down the side roads surrounding our town until the local diner's sign with a lit-up arrow points to my left. My stomach gurgles. I haven't eaten since breakfast. The parking lot is full, but I turn in anyway.

The scent of grilled burgers wafts through my open car window. My stomach growls louder. Once parked, I pull the car visor down and check the mirror. My eyes are red. The puffy skin underneath them, along with smudges of mascara streaking down my cheeks, has me frantically dabbing at my face with a tissue. Hunger pangs override my vanity. Maybe everyone inside will be too busy eating and visiting to notice I've been crying.

Shoulders back and posture straight, I sprint with long strides to the entrance. The bell attached to the glass door chimes when I enter, but thankfully, no one glances my way. The sign on a metal stand reads "Seat Yourself" in big, bold black letters. Before anyone notices me, I scuttle to a nearby booth and slump low into my seat.

A young waitress makes her way to my table with a menu and a glass of water in her hand. She looks familiar. Searching my memory, I picture a younger version of her running in a purple jersey. She was on the high school soccer team with Emma.

"Hi. Aren't you Emma's mom?" she asks with a sunny, youthful smile.

I divert my eyes to the menu she hands me, not wanting her to notice my red eyes. Then my conscience pricks. Not wanting to be rude, I plaster on a smile. Maybe she will only think I'm tired. "Yes, I am." My chirpy voice sounds fake to my ears.

I had hoped to be in and out of this diner without engaging in small talk, but Emma's old schoolmate wants to chitchat.

"How's Emma doing?"

"Oh, she's doing well," I say in a happy singsong tone while feeling dismal on the inside. Before she has time to ask any more about Emma, I blurt out, "What's the special?"

"Taco salad." She points to the chalkboard menu on the wall.

I hand her the menu. "I'll have the taco salad." I add a quick "water is fine" before she can ask anything else.

She writes my order on her notepad, then walks off. Relieved, I check my phone. No missed calls or texts from Emma or Dave. Probably for the best.

A boisterous group of ladies sits in a large circular booth behind me. I crane my neck their direction, trying to eavesdrop on their conversation. Howls of laughter intertwine with words like "Caesar's Palace ... gondola ride ... Cirque du Soleil."

When the waitress places my food on the table, my memory clicks. Ashley. The waitress' name is Ashley.

"Do you know the ladies behind me, Ashley?" I emphasize her name, praying my memory hasn't betrayed me. She doesn't correct me, so I add, "They seem to be having a fun time together."

"I don't." She bends closer to my face and whispers, "But I do know they are going on a girls trip to Las Vegas tomorrow. Doesn't that sound fun?" She winks.

"It does." When was the last time I did something fun?

The bell on the door jingles. Ashley leaves my table to greet the man and woman who are heading to a nearby booth. Thoughts of returning to my empty house have me picking at my meal. Even my appetite has abandoned me. After placing my napkin over my plate, I drag myself out of the booth to pay my bill.

More laughter spills from behind me, and pain tweaks my heart. They seem to be having the best time. Compelled, I turn toward the circular booth. Three women—seventy-ish, by my guess—sit with flushed faces. A wistful smile forms as I watch the group of ladies enjoying each other's company. Dreading returning home, I do something out of character. I walk to their booth.

The conversation stops as they stare up at me.

Hot flames shoot up my neck. What am I doing? "I'm so sorry. I'm usually not this forward," I say, flustered. "You see, I was at the cash register, and you ladies seemed to be having such a good time, and ..." I run my hands down my crinkled shirt to smooth out the wrinkles. "You're going to think I'm crazy, but I felt drawn to meet you." My pulse pounds as I wait for their reaction. Will they burst into more laughter or tell me to leave? Maybe both.

Neither happens. Instead, the woman with the tight gray curls says, "Well then, you must sit with us. We were just getting ready to order some pie."

Dumbfounded, I stare like she has two heads, but she doesn't seem to notice.

"I'm Agnus." Her warm, pleasant voice slows my pulse. "These are my friends Bea and Delores." Each lady nods at me as Agnus says their names.

"It's nice to meet you all. I'm Sarah."

Delores pats the seat next to her.

"I should go." I push my purse strap to my shoulder but hesitate to leave.

Agnus's warm brown eyes, made larger by her horn-rimmed silver glasses, rest on my face. "You look tired, Sarah. Have some pie with us. My treat."

"Yes, please do," Bea says in a deeper tone. Her lime-green polyester athletic suit reminds me of my elementary school gym teacher.

Delores pats the seat again. "Whatever you're going through, pie always helps. At least that's our motto." They all laugh again, and she winks at me through her black rhinestone-framed glasses.

Taking a deep breath, I concede and slide into the booth beside Delores.

"Yay!" The ladies' cheer causes several heads to turn toward us.

My face again heats from the attention while a blanket of warmth spreads across my heart. The tension in my shoulders eases as I listen to them. I'm thankful for the distraction from the events of today.

We place our pie orders and add coffee.

"We are in a pickle," Agnus says as soon as Ashley leaves, and the other ladies nod.

Raising an eyebrow, I wait for Agnus to continue.

"We booked a trip to Las Vegas for four people," she states. "But only three of us can go."

"What happened?" I ask.

Each lady leans in, making our circle tighter.

"Our friend Irene was our fourth. She fell trying to put shingles on her roof and broke her hip," Agnus explains.

"Why she was on her roof, I will never understand." Delores purses her ruby-red lips.

"Don't you ladies know what happened?" Bea lifts her cloth napkin to the side of her mouth to conceal her words from the neighboring tables. "Instead of getting a friend to help him fix her roof, her good-for-nothing son had Irene on the roof with him." She smacks her palm on the table. A vein in her temple pulses.

"Well, it's not all his fault." Delores's numerous bracelets clang and sparkle with each movement of her wrist. "Irene always thinks she's younger than she really is—trying to do things she knows she shouldn't be doing—acting like she's twenty when she's eighty-two."

Agnus nods. Her gray curls jiggle.

"You know that's true." Bea nods her baseball-capped head.

"What's worse, Irene has been saving for this trip all year, and now she can't go. She tried to get her money back from the travel agency, but they said it was too late. They have a thirty-day no-refund policy. It's a shame. I'm sure she could use that money for her medical bills." Agnus tsks.

All three women stop talking, seemingly lost in their own thoughts, as Ashley unloads our desserts and coffees from her tray onto the table.

"I could buy the ticket," I blurt out.

# CHAPTER FOUR

"I'm sorry. I shouldn't have invited myself along. You don't even know me." I look down at my hands, the surge of energy that ran through my body a moment ago now replaced with heaviness. "It's a crazy idea. I don't even know why I suggested it." My shoulders droop. "It's not like me to do something so bold or spontaneous."

"I love it," Delores shouts beside me.

My head snaps up, and my gaze darts over to Delores.

Her sky-blue eyes gleam. Bea and Agnus turn to look at her too.

"Why not?" Delores directs her attention to her friends. "The money for the ticket will help Irene—and maybe Sarah too." Delores shifts her focus to me. "There's a reason we met you tonight. Wouldn't it be fun to find out what that is?"

Bea and Agnus shrug, then nod. All three ladies smile at me, causing a wave of exhilaration to pulse through my veins.

Agnus grabs her purse, then pulls out a paper outlining the details of the trip with a ticket attached.

Before I start reasoning why I can't go, I hand her a check.

Bea pulls out her phone. "Let's exchange phone numbers."

Every word of caution I've ever given to Emma regarding "stranger danger" appears front and center in my mind, but I ignore the rules and give them my number.

Numbers exchanged, we gather our items and rise from the booth.

"Meeting adjourned." Delores giggles.

"You better go pack," Agnus says.

Bea pats me on the back. "Yes, we leave bright and early."

Once outside, I sit in my car, watching them leave one by one. Shaking my head in disbelief, I shift into drive and head back home.

# CHAPTER FIVE

T he house is pitch black when I pull the car into our driveway. It's hard to believe a few hours earlier I was walking Emma down this same sidewalk, making different plans. With a slow twist of the key and a push on the front door, the crater in my heart expands as I survey the empty living room.

I flip on the lights in every room except Emma's. With all the remodeling in the past year, the house doesn't look like home anymore. All new painted walls, flooring, and furniture fill the house now. The only room left untouched is Emma's bedroom. Thinking she would be here this summer, her last one at home, I didn't want to change a thing.

A wave of nausea overtakes me when I remember the ticket in my purse. What was I thinking? I can't go on this trip. I have too much to do to leave on such short notice. Searching for evidence to support my logic, I march into the kitchen and pull the calendar free from the wall. Each blank square contradicts my excuses. I have no appointments scribbled down for this month. My face scrunches in denial. That can't be right.

Fresh pain tweaks my heart. I sink onto the kitchen chair, my brain trying to produce any plausible reason not to go on this trip. Imagine the mess my house will be in when I get back. Who will make Dave's dinner or take his clothes to the dry cleaner? I jerk upright. *Just because the calendar is empty doesn't mean I'm not busy.* I smack the table with the palm of my hand.

The grandfather clock in the hallway chimes twelve times. It's midnight. I've been debating whether or not to go on this trip for a good two hours. Berating myself for taking so long to decide, I give in to sensible logic. The weight on my chest grows heavy as I accept my decision—I'm not going. I'm being ridiculous.

I rise to trudge over to the sink to wash a pan soaking in the water I'd left there earlier. I place the stopper in the drain and watch the last of my dish soap dribble and sputter into the lukewarm running water. My husband's forgotten cell phone dings on the kitchen table.

I dry my hands on a dish towel and cross over to the table where his phone rests faceup. Emma's picture fills the screen. Warning bells ring in my head. Why is she texting her dad so late? Is she okay? Has something happened? She needs me. Taking a few breaths to ramp down my habitual panic response, I click the passcode that opens his phone.

Dad, are you there?

My fingers tap over the phone's keyboard with rapid speed.

This is your mom. Your dad forgot to take his phone with him. Is everything okay?

Three bubbles appear, then disappear. The moments

waiting for her to respond have my imagination spinning images of Emma lying in a ditch somewhere.

After what seems an eternity but is probably less than a minute, she responds.

Yes, everything is fine, Mom.

I can hear her scolding tone on the word *Mom*, knowing she thinks I'm being overprotective as always.

After a beat, another text comes through.

I had a question for Dad. It can wait until he gets home from his trip.

The words sting a little, but I swallow them down. I text back a simple response.

Okay.

While waiting for Emma to text a goodbye, good night, love you, anything, I notice a long thread of texts between her and Dave. A mental debate ensues as I stare at the screen. Several minutes pass, making it clear Emma's done with our conversation.

I should put the phone down and head to bed, but instead, I continue to grip the cell. I shouldn't read their conversation. It's wrong. My head nods in agreement, but flashes of past hurts from feeling like the "odd man out" whenever Emma and Dave are together have my right index finger scrolling to the beginning of their conversation.

Are you sure you have to tell your mom tonight?

Yes, I'm sure.

I won't be home when you tell her. I should be there.

I know, Dad, but I need to tell her
tonight.

        She's going to be upset. You know that,
        right?

Mom will be okay. It will all work out.
You'll see.

        I don't know. You might just break her
        heart.

Throwing the phone down on the kitchen table, I scream, "Mom is not okay." My chest tightens, making it difficult to breathe. Emma cut me out of one of the most important events in her life. Her father knew about the elopement. He gave Emma and Philip his blessing while keeping me in the dark.

*Get a life!* His words come crashing down on me again. A small flame sparks into a burning inferno in my chest. Heat rises to my face. Get a life? I'll show you, Dave Goodwin.

Grabbing the calendar from the table, I stomp over to the junk drawer and pull out a red sharpie. In big, bold letters, I write GETTING A LIFE across the empty spaces. With a flourish, I hang it back on the wall. Then I pull the trip itinerary from my purse and scribble a brief note at the top. I sign it, "It will all work out, Sarah" and prop it against the floral centerpiece on the table. He can't miss it.

Fueled by anger, I'm unable to think about what needs to be done next. I count—one, two, three, four—breathing in and out to clear my head. Clarity returns. After stomping to our bedroom, I pull out my suitcase and throw it on the bed. Some of the adrenaline subsides as I stare at my suitcase, stumped, not knowing what to pack. Maybe I should look at the itinerary? I know we are headed to Vegas, but I don't know if there will be other stops or how many days we will be gone. After a few moments contemplating whether to go back to the kitchen to read the itinerary, I question if I really care where we're going. The answer is a big fat no. Anywhere is better than here.

I ransack my closet, throwing in shirts, tees, capris, long pants, shorts, and two pairs of shoes. Last, I toss a dress into the overfull suitcase, hoping there's not a weight limit.

Now for the toiletries. What a name for hygiene and makeup products. I roll my eyes as I walk to our bathroom vanity. As I fill the carry-on bag, my reflection draws my attention.

My formerly straightened hair now curls in random places from the humidity and heat of the day. I try to smooth my hair back down, but the natural auburn waves rebel against the pressure of my hands. Shrugging, I set my straightener beside my makeup bag to pack in the morning, then walk back to our bedroom. Scanning the room for anything else I might need, my eyes settle on the framed picture sitting on the dresser. In the photo taken twelve years ago, Emma sits on my lap flashing a big cheesy smile, even though she's missing two upper front teeth. Light-brown freckles pepper her nose and cheeks. Her long black hair is pulled up into a ponytail with a big red bow. Dave stands behind us. Leaning down with his arms around our shoulders, he huddles us close in a snug bear hug. His smile reaches his warm mocha-colored eyes, forming happy crinkle lines beside them. His hair is black as coal, not having grayed yet. Emma is his carbon copy.

My heart melts. Nostalgia replaces outrage. My mind drifts to happier memories, bringing up a list of Dave's wonderful attributes as a father and husband. But I stop myself, not wanting to give into sentimentality. I remind myself how angry I am with him right now. Whether Dave wants to believe it or not, he messed up.

My eyes shift from Dave and Emma to me. I pick up the

picture and hold it next to my face. I lean closer to the dresser mirror and compare the younger version of me to my reflection. Crow's feet now spread outward from my green eyes where smooth, taut skin used to be. Lines now form a parenthesis around my lips, and permanent worry wrinkles crease between my eyebrows. Skin sags underneath my chin. Placing the photograph back in its place on the dresser, I raise my hands to my face, lifting and pulling, attempting to tighten my loose skin. As soon as I drop my hands, all the wrinkles and sagging appear again, proving my efforts pointless. No amount of collagen or miracle beauty creams can make me look like the younger version of myself.

Sighing, I glance once more at the photo. *Where did the time go?* I thought I had more. Misty-eyed, I carry my large bag to the living room.

Satisfied I'm ready for the trip, I walk back to our bedroom to lie down, hoping for a few hours of sleep. Instead of rest, I toss and turn, my mind whirling.

A thought pushes its way to the forefront. I never put my wedding dress away. I tiptoe toward the living room, then shake my head. There's no one here to wake up. I can stomp if I want to. So I do—all the way to the recliner.

The dark-gray garment bag lies across the couch cushions. I gather the dress, then lay it inside the bag. Before tucking it away, I gingerly trace my fingers over the lace-and-pearl beading on the neckline. The back of my throat burns as I run the zipper up, closing the bag until its contents are hidden away.

Exhaling a deep sigh, I plod to Emma's room to hang it in her closet. Upon opening her door, I'm greeted by a beautiful sunrise shining through her bedroom window. A stream of light makes an aisleway across her plush pink carpet. Emma's white canopied four-poster bed holds an array of forgotten stuffed animals stacked on her pillows. A kaleidoscope of mental images swirl—us cuddled together when she was little, reading children's books and singing silly songs, accompanied by the distant echo of Emma's giggles.

I veer my focus away from the bed to trod over to her closet. Opening the door, I push aside the assortment of formal dresses Emma wore during high school. I shut my eyes for a moment, breathing in deeply the lingering scent of her perfume, then hang the wedding dress next to the other formal garments. My vision blurs.

A woodpecker bangs its beak on the windowpane, bringing me back to the present. It's morning. I sigh into the quiet. Time to get ready. Time to get a life.

Nervous energy takes over. I stride back to my bedroom. Makeup applied, I throw on my favorite blue-jean capris, a comfortable top, and sandals, then finish packing my carry-on bag. Straightening my unruly hair takes the longest, leaving little time for breakfast.

The grandfather clock chimes six times. The bus leaves at seven. I walk through the house once more before retrieving my bags. Nausea hits the pit of my stomach again, but this time, it's accompanied by an unexpected rush of excitement. I survey the living room, ensuring all physical reminders of what transpired yesterday are gone. The corner of a Polaroid picture sticks out from under the recliner. It must have landed there when I dropped the box of photos yesterday and was hidden by the train of my wedding dress.

I grab the photo off the floor, then check my watch. Since I don't have enough time to return the picture to the box in the basement, I throw it into my purse, grab my bags, and walk out the door.

# CHAPTER SIX

I steer my SUV into the travel company's parking lot. A big blue bus with the company's logo looms large on the black asphalt. When I pull my vehicle around to the right side of the bus, I see a long line of women in single file handing over their luggage to a man in a navy-blue uniform. My chest tightens. Am I making a huge mistake? Before my thoughts begin to spiral, the ladies I met at the diner descend on me.

Bea, now in a purple polyester jogging suit, opens my door. She grabs my left hand, tugging it until she pulls me out of the car and onto my feet. "Where are your bags, dear? We don't want to be late boarding the bus."

I swallow hard and point to the back of my vehicle.

Before I have an opportunity to jump back in and peel out of the parking lot, Agnus, Bea, and Delores take quick strides to the back of my SUV, leaving me standing at the driver's side door. Agnus opens the hatch, lifts out my bags, and sets them on the pavement. Bea grabs the rolling suitcase and quickly glides it to the uniformed man loading luggage.

Delores throws my smaller bag over her shoulder,

motioning me to follow. The numerous bangles on her wrists jingle with each step she takes toward the waiting bus.

Wide-eyed, I stare at their backs as they carry off my belongings. Wondering whether to follow them or jump back in my automobile and drive away, I'm immobilized. Agnus, Bea, and Delores have almost made it to the bus when Delores looks over her shoulder.

I haven't moved from where they left me. The impulse to escape grows stronger.

Delores gives me a warm, patient smile and walks back to me. Heat rises to my neck when she takes my hand and leads me to the end of the passenger line.

Once we reach the uniformed man, he grabs my suitcase, throws it in the underbelly of the bus, then pulls down the large door. It slams and locks into place, and I jump. Delores moves behind me at the bus steps, placing herself between me and the path to my car.

Once inside, my eyes take in the laughing and exuberant senior ladies. A strong mixture of various perfumes fills the air. Agnus and Bea seat themselves in the second row on the left. Delores motions me to the empty spots across the aisle from them. I scrunch in first, seating myself by the window so they can visit.

With the bus loaded, the uniformed man takes a seat behind the steering wheel. He plops a navy-blue hat onto his silver hair. Another man enters the bus. He looks fortyish—around the same age as Dave and me. He and I are probably the youngest people on this bus. While this man is tall, Dave is taller. He wears a burgundy polo with the travel agency's logo embroidered on the upper front left side, paired with khaki pants and brown shoes.

He picks up a handheld microphone from the front seat. A loud *thump, thump, thump* sounds over the speakers as he taps it. "Testing one, two, three." His baritone voice follows. The man picks up a clipboard from the front seat, juggling it and the microphone, until he has a good grip on both. "Hi. My name is Bob, and I will be your motor-coach guide."

"Hi, Bob," some ladies in the back yell. Giggles erupt from several women.

Red-faced, he waves, clears his throat, then reads a list of instructions attached to the clipboard. When he finishes, he raises his blond head and asks, "Are there any questions?" When none of the ladies reply, he nods, then moves another sheet of paper to the top of the stack. "When I call your name, please raise your hand."

One by one, Bob calls out names. His dark-blue eyes search the busload of ladies, waiting for raised hands. So far, everyone seems to be accounted for. "Irene Stapleton." This time no one raises their hand. He scrunches his eyebrows and narrows his eyes. "Irene Stapleton?" I twist around in my seat. Everyone scans the area around them, whispering as they search for the missing passenger.

I'm mortified. Agnus, Bea, Delores, or Irene didn't inform the travel agency about the change in tickets. I snap my head their direction, hoping they will speak up, but they seem oblivious the travel director called for their friend. They're engaged in a conversation about a host of people chasing a runaway pig at their county fair.

"Irene Stapleton, please raise your hand," Bob repeats in a frustrated tone.

I wince, then raise my hand halfway.

"Are you Irene?" he asks through gritted teeth.

"Irene couldn't come, so we brought Sarah Goodwin instead," Agnus shouts as she points at me.

I'm thankful she finally spoke up, but the weight of

numerous eyes boring into my back makes me want to hide under my seat. My face flushes with embarrassment.

The travel director crooks his index finger, motioning me to come forward.

Slowly, I stand and walk to the front of the bus. Flustered, I summarize the events of last night at the diner, leaving out the parts about Dave and Emma.

He stands with one hand on his hip and the other gripping the clipboard and microphone, listening but never saying a word.

I finish with, "And that's how I ended up here."

Bob sets the clipboard and microphone down on the front seat, then turns back to face me. I stand stiff, waiting to be kicked off the bus.

Conflicting emotions cross his face before he speaks. "It's not that I don't want you to come with us, but this isn't your reservation. You didn't sign up for this trip. How do I know Irene Stapleton willingly gave up her seat? Do you have a receipt for the purchased ticket? Have you filled out the proper paperwork? We need your emergency contacts and insurance information."

Rattled and humiliated for my impulsive decision, I turn to retrieve my purse. A wall of bodies stops me, standing unmoving, blocking my path—Agnus, Bea, and Delores. I gulp.

Agnus moves around me, placing herself between Bob and me. "Bob, is it?" With her index finger, she taps the name tag pinned on his shirt.

Bob takes a step back, then says, "Yes, ma'am."

Delores scoots around me too. She has a red blinged-out cell phone in her hand. "Here's Irene. She can tell you she's fine with Sarah taking her place."

Bob shakes his head, but Delores continues to wave it at him. With a loud sigh, he takes the phone. "Hello, ma'am. This is Bob Thurman and ..." He holds the phone a few inches from his ear. The incessant, loud voice on the other end is unintelligible to me, but Bob's face reddens in response. His lips close in a grim line.

After a few moments, the line goes quiet. Bob takes this opportunity to say, "Uh-huh, yes, ma'am. I totally understand, but it's against company policy."

A stream of words again blares from the other end of the line. Bob rubs the back of his neck while continuing to listen. After several more minutes, he groans. "Okay, we will work something out, ma'am. Goodbye." With his index finger, he dramatically taps the "end call" button and hands the phone back to Delores.

"Mrs. Irene Stapleton confirmed what you said, but there is still the matter of filling out the necessary forms." He stabs the clipboard with his finger.

"Can't she fill out the forms along the way?" Agnus challenges.

Bea pushes me forward in the crowded aisle until I'm face-to-face again with Bob. "Just look at her," Bea shouts. "Can't you see how badly she needs this trip?"

I cringe inside, wishing I could—*poof*—disappear.

"I would need to go back into the office." He checks his watch. "We are already behind schedule." His eyes bore into mine. "I'm sure the rest of the passengers are more than ready to get going." He cranes his head above Bea, Delores, Agnus, and me to glance at the other travelers who have been watching our little drama play out.

"If she can't come, none of us are going," Delores declares.

I suck in air, feeling the color drain from my face. I swing around to gape at her. The phrase "tiny but mighty" comes to mind at the sight of her set jaw, her feet planted firmly in the aisle, and her arms crossed over her chest.

Bea adds, "Yeah, and forget about a good Yelp review."

Agnus nods in agreement.

I want to tell them all this fuss is unnecessary, but I am speechless.

"Let her come!" A low chant starts from the back of the bus, then grows louder until the whole bus is chanting, "Let her come! Let her come!"

In disbelief, I look past my new acquaintances to the other women. They don't even know me, yet they're all cheering for me. Astonished, I wait for Bob's decision.

"Can you believe this, Frank?" he asks the bus driver.

Frank smiles, shrugs, then pulls the lever to open the door.

"Et tu, Brute?" Bob glares at the ceiling, throws his hands up in the air, and descends the stairs.

The ladies seated on the left move to peer over the women on the right side of the bus and watch Bob stomp across the parking lot. From the open windows, we can hear him mumbling, "Be a tour director. It will be fun, they said."

The whole bus erupts with laughter.

Bob swings around. Red-faced, he stares at us with sullen annoyance. Most of the ladies quiet down. Only a few giggles can be heard through covered mouths. Raising his chin, Bob pivots, then scuttles across the parking lot and disappears into the travel agency.

The ladies return to their seats. Only Delores, Bea, Agnus, and I remain standing as we wait for Bob.

I'm still at the front of the line, so close to the open door that adrenaline surges down my legs. The impulse to run off the bus before Bob returns tempts me. Just as I'm reaching back to grab my purse, Delores loops her arm through mine, foiling my escape. She winks at me, then her lips form a mischievous smile. Did she know what I was thinking, or did my look of desperation give me away?

44

Huffing and scowling all the way back from the travel agency, Bob reenters the bus. He hands me the forms, then shoos us to our seats. "Off you go."

Before turning away, I mouth, "I'm so sorry."

He doesn't answer, but his facial expression softens.

Once we're back in our seats, Frank closes the door. The bus lurches forward.

"Yay! We're on our way," a loud, high-pitched voice yells from the back. All the ladies cheer.

My neck and shoulders relax with the rhythmic drumming of the wheels on the pavement.

"In a few short hours, we cross the Kansas state line," says Delores.

A memory of Emma's sweet little-girl voice replays in my mind. "We're tourists now, Momma." She clapped as we left the Missouri state line. My lips curve upward into a bittersweet smile.

Delores grabs my hand and gives it a little squeeze. "Penny for your thoughts."

She's too perceptive. I glance at her but avoid making eye contact. "I'm wondering if I did the right thing, coming on this trip."

"I know it was a little rough getting started, but it will be smooth sailing from now on." Her tone and soothing manner make me want to believe, but a nagging reminder follows. Dave will be home soon.

# CHAPTER SEVEN

Pretending to read, I peak over the top of my magazine and watch the ladies talk back and forth. Who are these women who befriended me?

Agnus glances my way, smiles, then returns her attention to Bea. I remember Agnus the most from our encounter last night. She has soft brown eyes framed by horn-rimmed glasses and short gray permed hair that jiggles when she talks. She wears a pair of cropped white pants with a red, white, and blue-striped tee. Aside from the simple gold wedding band on her left ring finger, she's jewelry free.

Bea has removed her purple jogging jacket, revealing a plain white tee. She has black mesh slip-on sneakers. Her reddish-brown bangs poke out from under her purple ball cap. Bea catches me staring at her.

Beads of sweat pepper my upper lip. I give her a timid smile, then lift my magazine, hiding my face. After waiting until I think it's safe, I lower the magazine again. Bea's focused on Agnus and their conversation, so I breathe a sigh of relief.

Checking out my seat partner is trickier. I snatch glances

at her while continuing to pretend I'm reading. Her closed eyes allow me an opportunity for a longer look. Delores's jet-black hair is cut into a short layered bob. With her chin tucked to her chest, her black rhinestone eyeglasses are perched halfway down her nose. She's an impeccable dresser. Her red blazer over a cream top and black dress slacks are more appropriate for an interview than a bus trip. Even though her ruby-red lipstick has faded, the color still matches her blazer. Then there's the jewelry. Multi-strand gold layered necklaces hang around her neck. With each bump or turn in the road, big hoop earrings sway below her ears. Her diamond rings catch the sunlight, sparkling every time she moves her hands, while gold and silver bangles jingle around her wrists. It must take her a good hour to put her jewelry on each morning. Last, I glance down at her bright-red toenails peeking out from tall cream wedges. How does she walk in those shoes? The heel must be at least four inches. Maybe more. I hope this trip doesn't include a lot of walking, for her sake.

"You're not going to rob me, are you?" Delores asks, her eyes still closed.

My head snaps up. I gasp, embarrassed she caught me giving her a once-over.

"No." I pause, trying to think how to explain. "S-sorry. I-I'm just trying to figure things out."

A thundering laugh erupts from her. I'm surprised the booming sound came from such a small body. Removing her glasses, she shifts to study me. Her sky-blue eyes penetrate mine. They're beautiful but a little intimidating.

"When you figure things out, let me know. I might need to know things too." She chuckles.

The bus veers right, taking an off-ramp. We've only been on the road for a short time. We can't be in Las Vegas already.

Since I didn't check out the itinerary, I have no idea where we are or why we are pulling off the highway.

After the bus makes a few twists and turns through the city streets, it stops, and then the passengers begin grabbing their belongings.

Bob stands to face us, no microphone in his hand this time. "Ladies, we are in Wamego, Kansas." His loud voice carries through the bus. "You have a few hours to walk around and have lunch. *The Wizard of Oz* annual festival is under way, so enjoy. You need to be back here on the bus in three hours." Pausing before pulling the lever to open the bus door, he shoots a glare directly at me. "And don't be late."

Delores snickers. "It's nice to not be the troublemaker for a change." She belts out another booming laugh when I grimace at her terrible joke.

Eager to stretch their legs, most of the ladies pass by us.

While we wait for our turn to exit the bus, I ask Delores, "Is the *Wizard of Oz* Museum here?"

"You really did have a rough night last night." She chuckles. "Didn't you read your itinerary?"

I wince. Embarrassment may be my constant companion on this trip.

"I take that as a no," she says, then winks at me.

As soon as our feet hit the pavement, we are greeted by a young teenage girl dressed as Dorothy and holding a Toto look-alike. I snap a picture of the two with my cell and send it to Emma.

> Look who I found. Can you guess where I am?

Memories of our annual tradition of watching *The Wizard of Oz* after returning home from trick-or-treating play in my mind. My throat thickens and my vision blurs as I remember the year I made Emma a Dorothy dress. She looked so sweet in her home-sewn blue-and-white gingham dress, with her black hair twisted into two braids and tied with matching gingham ribbons.

"Let's take a group photo." Bea's voice jolts me back to the present.

The young lady dressed as Dorothy waits for Delores and Agnus to join Bea.

I extend my hand to take Bea's cell, but she pushes it away. "You need to be in the photo too, Sarah."

Before I can protest, another lady from our bus says, "I'll take your picture."

Bea hands her the phone while I shuffle next to Delores. Agnus and Bea stand on one side of the look-alike Dorothy, and Delores and I on the other.

"Smile," the lady instructs. A series of snaps ensues, then she hands the phone back to Bea.

Other tourists stand in line, waiting for a picture with Dorothy, so we move out of their way. My cell dings. Hoping Emma's responding to the Dorothy picture I sent her, I grab it from my pocket.

The text isn't from her. My mind begins to spiral with my usual sour thoughts that come from being ignored, but then I see the notification's from Bea. It's our group picture. I pinch the screen to enlarge it. Someone who didn't know us might look at this picture and assume we've been lifelong friends. Our smiles are big and bright, even mine. The awkwardness from this morning is now replaced by a sense of camaraderie. Belonging. I'm not sure I can trust the foreign feeling of inclusion, but for the moment, I'll enjoy it.

"What should we do first?" Agnus asks.

The museum on the right is a replica of the emerald-green

castle from the movie. Across from the museum lies a pathway between buildings—a yellow brick road.

My eyes grow wide. I want to break into a run toward it, but I hold myself back. Delores smiles at my reaction. Looping her arm in mine, she leads us to the brick road. Agnus and Bea follow.

When my left foot hits the first brick, I pause and glance at Delores.

"Go ahead. You know you want to." Deloris releases my arm.

I take off skipping my way to the end of the path, lighter than I have been in a long time.

Bea follows, skipping halfway down the path, then stops and doubles over. "No, I'm good," she huffs, out of breath.

Once we return to Agnus and Delores, we walk to the museum, pay our admission, and begin Dorothy's journey. In the first room, a life-sized wax figure of Dorothy holds tight to "her little dog," Toto. There's a mural painted on the wall behind her of a Kansas farm with a large, looming black funnel cloud in the distance. From the speaker system, shouts of Auntie Em calling out to Dorothy are intertwined with the roar of the Kansas tornado headed their way. Agnus and Bea stop, then walk on to the next scene. Delores stays back with me.

Even though this replica of Dorothy is made of wax, her pained expression resonates with something sorrowful in my core. She's realizing her world is spinning out of control, and there's nothing she can do to stop it.

"A pretty intense situation, wouldn't you say?" Delores studies the scene, then glances at me. I nod. She asks, "Have you ever been in a tornado?"

Before thinking, I say, "Yes, the night I met you in the diner."

She releases an uncomfortable laugh, and my face heats. I shouldn't have said that out loud.

We continue through the museum, taking group selfies with wax figures of the Scarecrow, Tin Man, Cowardly Lion, and Wicked Witch of the West. The last room houses a duplicate of the hot-air balloon that transported the Wizard back to Kansas, unexpectedly leaving Dorothy behind. A young man working the exhibit helps us into the basket for a picture.

"Smile," he says.

I muster a melancholy smile while holding back tears. Sometimes you can't go home again, at least not the home you long for.

Bea touches my shoulder. "Are you all right, Sarah?"

I scrunch up my face. "Yes, just allergies."

Bea tilts her head, eyeing me longer than feels comfortable.

A line of people is waiting to have their pictures taken in the basket. The young man who assisted us points to the exit, giving me a way out of this conversation.

The souvenir shop is strategically placed at the exit. We all scatter to find a trinket or knickknack to remember our visit here. A charm in the shape of the famous ruby-red slippers twinkles from where it hangs on the wall. I pull one down from the pegboard and hold red glitter and a silver sparkle in my palm.

"'You've always had the power, my dear, you just had to learn it for yourself.'" Delores stands behind me as she quotes the famous line from Glinda the Good Witch.

I smile at her, then take the charm to the counter, excited to make my first purchase on this crazy adventure.

Delores follows me to the cashier's line, holding a coffee cup that reads, "Don't make me get my flying monkeys."

I laugh and shake my head.

Agnus files in behind Delores. In her hands, she holds "I'm

Melting" hand lotion and a small license plate that reads, "My other car is a broom."

Bea meets us at the door, already wearing her new souvenir. Her purple hat from earlier has been replaced with a rhinestone-studded emerald-green ball cap with *The Wizard of Oz* Museum logo embroidered in bright yellow-and-purple thread on the front.

"I'm starving," Bea announces. "You girls want to get some lunch?"

My stomach growls, confirming it's time to eat.

Exiting the museum, we walk down the sidewalk, past several gift shops, and into a little diner.

After we're seated in a booth, we peruse the menu. All the food platters are named after *Wizard of Oz* references.

When the waitress arrives, Bea orders the red slipper meal —a pasta with red sauce, better known as spaghetti. "I'll have the Over the Rainbow taco salad," I say. The menu describes it as a mound of multicolored tortilla chips topped with ground beef, nacho cheese, and jalapenos.

"The munchkin breakfast for me," says Agnus. It's a stack of pancakes covered in apple syrup. A rainbow-colored fruity lollipop stands on the top of the stack.

Delores orders a healthier option—the Wizard's greens—a chef salad.

We chuckle as we pass our menus to the waitress.

Still a little emotional from earlier, I let sentiment override my usual private nature. Before I lose my nerve, I say, "I want to thank you for including me today. It meant a lot that you allowed me to buy your friend's ticket, but I never expected you'd actually want me to come along." Tears build behind my eyes, so I pause to compose myself. "I thought once I got on the bus, I would be on my own. I was okay with that, but please don't feel like you have to entertain or include me in everything. I'm grateful for all you've done so far." I stop rambling and hold my breath, searching their faces for a reaction.

Agnus smiles in a gentle, motherly way. "We love having you with us, Sarah."

Bea adds, "We knew when we met that you were one of us."

Humbled, I wait for Delores's response. Instead of saying something sweet or kind like Agnus and Bea, she howls in laughter. "We couldn't get rid of you if we wanted." She slaps the table. "You're rooming with us."

Agnus and Bea join in her bursts of laughter.

"I am?" I ask, wide-eyed.

Delores winks.

"I should've looked at the information you gave me, Agnus."

The ladies howl more. Several customers in nearby booths look at us. My companions' laughs are contagious.

I ignore the onlookers and laugh too, quiet at first, but then it builds until tears stream down my face. "What have I gotten myself into?"

Before leaving, we finish our meal with our customary pie. Of course, we all get apple. The menu claims it's made from the same apples thrown at Dorothy in the Haunted Forest of Oz.

Agnus checks her watch. "Oh my. It's time to go."

We were having so much fun, we lost track of the time.

"Bob will be after you, Sarah." Delores winks again.

I grin and open my eyes wide, feigning fear.

We grab our purses and souvenirs, leaving the half-eaten slices of pie, then dash to the waiting bus. Bob stands at the entrance, pointing at his watch. We scamper up the stairs and plop into our seats.

Clipboard in hand, Bob takes roll. Once he says my name, I

relax and watch the people outside my window. My gaze lands on a young mom and a little girl sitting on a bench and eating small cups of ice cream. The girl squirms—full of energy—as she talks to her mom. The mom seems to be enjoying the conversation as well. Both share smiles between bites of their ice cream.

Memories of Emma at that age have my throat burning again. She used to love going everywhere with me—my constant companion. She kept me entertained, too, always sharing funny stories about her day. What I wouldn't give to relive one of those days with her.

Delores interrupts my brooding. "Oh, before I forget, I bought you a bracelet at the museum gift shop for your charm."

I take the charm from my souvenir bag and slide the ruby-red slipper onto the sterling-silver serpentine bracelet.

She motions me to hold out my arm, so I do. She drapes the bracelet around my wrist, shortening the length with the sliding clasp until it fits. The sunlight catches the charm so that it twinkles when I hold it closer to my face.

Hugging the bracelet to my heart, I say, "Thank you, Delores. I love it."

She beams. "To new friendships, new memories, and new beginnings."

# CHAPTER EIGHT

I'm surprised when we open the door to our first motel room. It only has two full-sized beds. There are no couch pullouts or rollaway beds. Realization hits me—I'm sharing a bed with one of these ladies.

I'm sure this was listed in the trip details I left back home. It wouldn't be so awkward if Irene had made the trip, but now one of the ladies has to share a bed with a woman they met last night. I keep quiet, listening to the ladies list the pros and cons of each sleeping arrangement. After a long discussion of who sleeps with who, they decide it's best if I share a bed with Delores.

The room is small, but the sink counter is outside the bathroom. One of us can shower while another brushes her teeth. It takes some maneuvering, but finally we have all washed our faces, brushed our teeth, and put on our pajamas.

Agnus and Bea take the bed nearest the door, leaving Delores and me the bed by the wall. Delores settles on the right side. She fluffs and pounds the motel pillow numerous times until she seems satisfied, then pulls the covers to her chin.

Asleep already, Agnus and Bea are oblivious to the flurry of activity in our bed.

Once I've settled on my side, Delores turns toward me and asks, "Comfy?"

"Yes, thank you," I reply.

She nods, then rolls away from me and faces the wall.

Inhaling and exhaling a few calming breaths, I close my eyes. I'm tired. Running away from home is exhausting. Just as my body starts to drift off to sleep, a loud noise startles me, then a low growl rumbles from Agnus's side of the bed, accompanied by a gravelly whistle from Bea. I remember that the deciding factor in our sleeping arrangements was that Agnus and Bea both snore. Delores does not. Our two beds are only a few feet away from each other, so did it really matter who I shared the bed with?

Dave snores. I've learned how to drown out the freight-train rumble he makes when he sleeps. I hum a tune in my head until I'm out. Most of the time it works. Before I can think of a tune to drown out the bellowing racket filling the room, Delores flops over and kicks me in the stomach.

"Ow." I'm surprised at the force of her kick. I rise onto my elbow to peek at her face. Her eyes are shut. I'm sure she didn't mean to kick me, but I turn my back to her in case she assaults me again.

She doesn't kick me again, but her arms and legs twist and flail in cyclonic motion. With each body roll, she takes the bedspread and sheets with her until she's wrapped up like a caterpillar in a cocoon. My body uncovered, I shiver while hugging the edge of the bed.

Remembering I draped my warm, fuzzy housecoat over a chair across the room earlier, I tiptoe over to retrieve it. I grab it and cover my body in its warmth. My shivering stops. Surely

Delores won't be able to rip this off me. I giggle quietly and climb back into bed.

Taking in deep breaths, I relax my muscles, starting with my toes and working up to my neck. I shut my eyes, and a song that my dad used to sing to me when I was little plays through my mind. The simple melody drowns out the snores coming from the other bed, allowing me to fall asleep.

* * *

Four cell phones blare with varying ringtones, waking me from a dream. Bea's alarm, louder than the others, plays "Bad to the Bone" by George Thorogood & The Destroyers. I bolt upright. Shaking my head, I take a moment to remember where I am.

Delores, Bea, and Agnus launch out of bed like they've been shot out of a cannon. A flurry of activity fills the small room. Not a morning person, I sit yawning, waiting for my turn to use the bathroom and change. I check my phone. There are several missed calls from Dave even though I sent him a text yesterday stating I was okay. I listen to his voicemails to make sure he and Emma are fine. He's ensured me they are. I know in my heart talking to him right now would not be good for either of us. I don't want to say something I'll regret.

With all of us sharing one small vanity, I fear there won't be enough time to do my hair and makeup. My brown leather crossbody sits on the nightstand next to my side of the bed. I carry a compact mirror in my purse. When I dump the bag's contents onto the bedspread, the compact falls out, along with the Polaroid picture I forgot about.

Delores walks to the bed and sits to put on her shoes. Busy applying makeup with the tiny mirror, I don't see her pick up the photo.

"Is this you, Sarah?" She flips it around to show me.

I continue putting on my makeup. "I'm not sure." I never looked at the photo.

I hope Delores will put the picture back and finish getting ready, but she continues to hold it. After brushing on some blush, I examine the photo. "Yes, that's me. I was probably four or five. Someone must have pulled my hair tight into two braids to make it lie down. In most of my childhood pictures, my hair looked like the Lucky Troll pencil toppers that used to be so popular. Do you remember those?"

Delores nods and chuckles.

"You were a cute little girl." She smiles and then hands me the photo.

Warmth rises from my heart into my cheeks. I never felt cute as a child.

Taking my eyes off the awkward little girl, I point at the picture. The tall blond man, grinning ear to ear, is standing next to me, holding my hand. "That's my dad." Pride wells in my chest.

Delores smiles. "He was a handsome man, but you don't look like him, do you? You must resemble your mom." She smiles again, examining my face. "I bet she's beautiful."

I shrug but blush at the compliment.

"Did she take the picture?" Delores asks.

"I'm not sure. I don't remember this photo. Probably because I was so young when it was taken." I shrug again, wishing she would quit with the questions.

"There's writing on the bottom. What does it say?" she asks.

I bring the photo closer to my face to read the faded handwriting. "The Grand Canyon—Seth and Sarah."

She bends down to buckle the straps on her shoes. "I've

never been to the Grand Canyon, but I've always wanted to go."

Bea belts out, "Sarah, it's your turn for the bathroom."

I shove the picture and the rest of the spilled contents back into my purse. Delores turns to the end table to put on her jewelry, and I escape to the bathroom before she can ask any more questions about my childhood.

I take my time getting dressed, waiting for my head to clear and my pulse to slow. I sigh, knowing it's time to rejoin the ladies. Opening the door, I'm met by Agnus, Delores, and Bea, wearing matching fluorescent-pink T-shirts that read, "Grandmas Gone Wild!" in sparkling silver letters.

Bea's tee is paired with a black athletic jacket and pants that she tucked into black cowboy boots. Agnus wears blue jeans tucked into white cowboy boots. Delores has a black leather jacket over her shirt with a pair of white dress pants tucked into pink rhinestone cowboy boots.

"Wow," I exclaim, not knowing what else to say.

"Sorry, Sarah. If we knew you were coming, we would have gotten you a tee to match," Agnus says.

"That's okay. I love your tees, but I'm not a member of the grandma club yet." I'm relieved I can make that statement. "My only child, Emma, just got married." My eyes prickle with tears.

"Congratulations," they cheer in unison.

"Thank you." I smile, warmed by their sincerity. Needing to change the subject before revealing my true feelings about the surprise wedding, I remind them, "We better get to our bus before Bob leaves us."

We grab our bags and dash from the room. Agnus and Bea walk ahead, chattering about who won some chili contest last year at their church. Delores and I trail behind.

Questions about Emma plague my mind. How's she doing? How's she handling married life? Are Philip and Emma doing okay financially? The most prominent thought, the one that replays on a continuous loop, is whether she is happy. A rogue tear slips down my cheek. I swipe at it with the back of my hand, hoping no one notices.

# CHAPTER NINE

"Breakfast? Check. Baggage loaded? Check. All ladies accounted for? Check." Bob waves his pen, and a satisfied smile spreads across his face. "Next stop, Dodge City."

Zealous shouts from the ladies fill the bus.

Our destination explains why my travel companions—along with several of the other women—are dressed in cowboy attire. I look out of place in my khaki cargo bermuda shorts, a navy tee, and tennis shoes.

Bob reads today's agenda and instructions, but he's lost everyone's attention as they talk and laugh with each other. He huffs, snaps off the mic, and plops onto his seat, then nods to Frank.

Frank moves the gear shift down and pulls the bus out of the parking lot, down a long ramp, and onto the windy Kansas highway.

Bea, Agnus, and Delores visit while I check my phone. No texts from Emma. Not even a response to the *Wizard of Oz* picture I sent yesterday. My heart sinks. Why does this void exist between us? How did it even begin?

I take a deep breath, then exhale, taking a beat before checking my phone again. A blue dot glows beside my husband's name. A new text from Dave. Hesitant, I tap on it. He sent only four words.

We need to talk.

The conversation we need to have can't happen with a bus full of women. I haven't had an opportunity to call him, or maybe I haven't created one. Dreading the conversation to come, I rather enjoy being like an ostrich with its head stuck in the sand.

Feeling guilty, I text back.

I'm on a bus headed to Dodge City.
Can't talk right now but will call you later.

That should buy me some time. Time for what? I don't know. Three dots appear on the screen. I wait for them to become words. They don't. After a few minutes, the dots disappear.

I try to relax, but my mind replays the conversation Dave and I had before he left for his business trip. Then there's the memory of Emma wiggling her fingers under my nose and telling me she eloped.

Lost in my thoughts, we've only been on the bus a short time when someone from the back shouts, "We're here!"

On the highway ahead of us, there's a life-sized cutout of seven cowboys riding horses, their lassos flying through the air. The metal sculpture stands on a rock wall. Hanging below it in big, bold black letters are the words "Dodge City."

Frank steers the bus into a parking lot next to the Boot Hill Cemetery. Beside it is the Fort Dodge jail. A sign above it reads, "Built about 1865."

Everyone scurries to exit the bus. While Bob gives us

instructions in the middle of the parking lot, my mind drifts to a different time.

I give free rein to my imagination, conjuring images of quarter horses and painted ponies tied to the hitching post beside the boardwalk as they drink water from the trough. Visions of cowboys, dusty from working cattle, walk up and down the dirt streets, while pioneer ladies dressed in floral prints shop and trade goods for their families' needs.

"And don't be late." Bob's customary shout ends my daydreaming.

The passengers scatter. Bea bolts for the Occident Saloon. The building's worn blue exterior with red trim reminds me of saloons I've seen in old western movies. Agnus, Delores, and I follow and push open the swinging brown oak doors.

Bea motions for us to sit on the tall wooden barstools. As we make our way to the bar, a man behind the counter grunts. "What will it be?" He has a long brown handlebar mustache, matching his slicked-back curly brown hair. He wears a brown vest over his white button-down shirt with blue sequenced bands around his biceps. A worn tan apron is tied around his waist.

"We will have four sarsaparillas, please," Bea orders, then giggles. She gives us a side glance. "I've always wanted to say that."

Delores and Agnus roll their eyes, but I grin, loving this game of make-believe.

The bartender brings over four caramel-colored glass bottles. Each time he pries the lid off a bottle using the edge of the bar, a loud *pop* ensues. Once the hiss dies down and the foam has finished spewing onto the bar, he hands a bottle to each of us. Bea takes the first swig. We watch, waiting for her reaction.

Confusion crosses her face, and then she scowls. "It tastes a lot like root beer," she says. "I don't like root beer."

"Well, I do." Delores chugs her sarsaparilla. She plops the bottle down on the counter, then wipes her mouth with the back of her hand. Her lipstick leaves a red streak across her knuckles.

My phone chirps inside my purse. The bartender frowns and points to the sign behind him that reads, "Cowboys don't have cell phones."

Before turning my phone off, I glance at the screen. Another missed call from Dave. Grimacing, I tuck the cell back into my purse.

Bea thumps her bottle twice on the bar. "Until next time." She waves at the bartender, signaling it's time to mosey on. We rise from our barstools. The ladies tip their hats before turning to leave.

I don't have a hat, so I shrug, grab my drink, then follow them through the swinging doors.

The ladies' boots *clip-clop* with every step they take on the wooden slatted sidewalks toward the City Drug and *Front Street Times* buildings. Inside the halls of the newspaper building, framed black-and-white photos and articles hang on the walls, along with historical documents displayed in locked glass cases.

All four of us stare at the numerous photos of people who helped settle the Kansas territory. The parents look older than their age from long days of hard work and worrying about having too little to feed their families. Children dressed in oversized hand-me-downs, with gaunt eyes and dirty faces, sit on their laps. The romanticized images I dreamed up while standing in the parking lot earlier are now replaced with sod houses, dirty, worn-out clothing, broken-down wagons, and weary faces.

"Hard times," Delores remarks, as if reading my mind.

Bea counters, "But people were a lot tougher back then."

Agnus nods. "They had to be."

"Although, families seemed a lot closer back then too," I say. "They lived in the same communities, gathering together to work the farm or share a meal." My voice rises, irritated. "I'm sure Laura Ingalls never told her ma, 'I'm too busy to come home.'"

Agnus, Bea, and Delores turn from the pictures and stare at me. Heat rises to my neck when I realize I expressed my thoughts out loud. I'm surprised I sounded so angry. I clear my throat, then move down the wooden hallway and away from their attention.

Gunshots ring outside. We scurry to the boardwalk.

Two groups of cowboys smack talk each other. To our right, a man with strands of shaggy brown hair peeking out from his black hat says, "Your boys rustled some cattle from my ranch." He makes a show of combing his bushy mustache and beard with his fingers, then places his hand on his holster.

A black-haired cowboy with a red bandana tied around his neck steps to the front of the other group. He squints, his hand on his holstered pistol, then snarls, "Do you have proof?"

The cowboys behind him snicker.

Those on the right side growl, then plant their legs in wide stances. They glare, shaking their fists with one hand and grabbing their holstered pistols with their other.

Both sides begin shooting. *Pop, pop, bang.* Smoke rises from the barrels of their guns. Some of the cowboys clutch at their chests before hitting the ground. Others run behind water troughs or wagon wheels, continuing to shoot at their enemies.

The parking lot is full of spectators. We watch as the two sides battle it out. The bearded cowboy finally takes down the one with the red handkerchief. His crew surrenders, their courage gone when their leader meets his demise. The "good" cowboys cheer and encourage the spectators to join them. Delores, Bea, and Agnus all hoot, throwing their hats in the air. Then the "dead" cowboys rise and join the live ones to form a line and take a bow. The audience claps.

Dave and Emma would hate this. I chuckle. Thinking of them reminds me of Dave's call. While Delores, Bea, and Agnus wait in line to get an autographed photo of the cowboys, I slip away to call him.

He answers after the first ring. "You finally returned my call. It's about time. I've been so worried."

"Well hello to you too," I say in a snarky tone.

"Why did you take off before giving me an opportunity to talk it through with you?" he shouts on the other end.

"By *it*, you mean Emma's elopement?" I surprise myself, my volume matching his.

"I wanted to tell you. Really, I did. I'm sorry she blindsided you the way she did. But that doesn't mean you should run off," he scolds.

"I'm angry at her for not talking to me about eloping, but I'm furious with you for keeping her secret," I lament. "You also said some hurtful things before you left. I always tried to be there for you and Emma. There were times I wanted to be someone other than Mrs. Goodwin or Emma's mom, but being a good wife and mother were more important. I guess I was wrong."

Dave doesn't answer. In the deafening silence, floorboards creak in the background of our home. He must be pacing across our kitchen.

My heart softens as I imagine the worry lines across his forehead. "I have to go. My *friends* are waiting on me." My voice becomes less shrill. "We are going to an Old West show."

"That doesn't sound like you," he replies.

"Well, isn't that the point?" I clench my teeth, wanting to throw my phone on the ground and smash it with my foot. "I'm making a new and improved me. Isn't that what you wanted? Friends? Check. What were the other things you told me to work on?"

A long silence follows. He releases a loud exhale. I picture him rubbing the back of his neck. "I'm sorry, Sarah. I didn't mean what I said." His voice is low and weary. "You're fine just the way you are."

"Yes, you did." Remembering his words still makes my heart ache.

"Sarah, be reasonable."

*Be reasonable?* My face heats. The urge to fire hurtful words at him tempts me, but the part that loves him holds me back. I take a deep breath to calm myself. "As hard as it was to hear your list of my shortcomings, you've given me a lot to think about. I'm not saying you're right. I just need time to work out some things in my head and my heart. Can you give me that?"

Agnus and Bea wave at me from a few buildings down. Delores motions me to join them. I nod, holding up my index finger. They give me a thumbs-up, then disappear into a forest-green building with a red-and-white insignia—"Long Branch Saloon"—painted above the weathered gray porch roof.

After a long pause, Dave says, "I guess I don't have a choice." His voice breaks. "Please remember, I love you."

Before I can reply, he hangs up.

"I know," I whisper.

# CHAPTER TEN

B linking back tears, I stare at the wooden planks beneath my feet. Slowly, I make my way to the big green building while asking myself why I am even here. I should go home and work things out with Dave.

Loud music blares from the open oak doors. I allow the crowd to push me along and through the entrance of the Long Branch Saloon. Young women dressed in lace-trimmed bodices attached to multicolored bell-shaped ruffled skirts greet the tourists entering the saloon. In the left corner of the room, a robust man hammers his fingers on black-and-white keys as loud chords explode from the antique piano. He wears a pink-striped button-down shirt with several multicolored garters on his forearms, and a pair of dusty black pants.

The cowboys from the gun-fight reenactment walk up and down the wooden floorboards, ushering people to their seats. Their spurs jingle with each step. The *pops* and *cracks* of the floorboards beneath their weight add an out-of-sync percussion to the rhythm of the piano.

"Over here, Sarah," Delores yells over the music and

chattering voices. She waves her hands like whirligigs. My friends have saved me a seat in the middle section to the left.

I make my way down the aisle through the tourists and actors. Agnus and Bea stand from their seats to let me through. Delores beams as the royal-blue crushed-velvet curtains rise. Her enthusiastic smile lifts my spirits.

*The Long Branch Variety Show*'s emcee is dressed in a black undertaker suit. He walks center stage to give his monologue. A tall black hat is perched sideways on his head. Groans from the audience grow louder with each corny joke and one-liner.

When the emcee finishes his set, he calls for the cancan girls. The same four young women who greeted everyone at the entrance now shuffle onto the stage.

The piano player's fingers hit hard in discord on the keys when he stops his song mid-tune. A tall, fiery red-haired woman, resembling Miss Kitty from *Gunsmoke*, enters from stage right. Her ankle-height, pointy black boots click with each step as she walks across the stage, seeming to assess the cancan girls. Big-eyed, the girls stand at attention.

She stops center stage and wags a finger at the emcee. "What did I tell you, Mr. Bailey?"

Mr. Bailey removes his too-large hat and rubs his white head of hair with his other hand. "I don't recall, Mamie Pearl." He winces.

Mamie Pearl shakes a fist at him. "I told you to hire more cancan girls. We can't do our routine with only four dancers."

Mr. Bailey smacks the side of his head. "I knew there was something I forgot."

"Now we can't do our dance for these nice folks." She extends her right arm, waving a blood-red manicured hand above the crowd. "I guess we'll have to refund their money."

"Refund their money?" Mr. Bailey shouts. After rubbing his stubbly white chin for several seconds, he snaps his fingers.

"I've got it." He lifts his right hand over his eyes to scan the audience. "Hey, I see some ladies that would make great cancan dancers."

Mamie Pearl's bright-red lips curve into a mischievous smile. Mr. Bailey points to the cowboys sitting on top of the bar. "Boys, go get some lady dancers."

The audience erupts.

"Yee-haw!" The cowboys jump down from the bar and clomp up and down the aisles, searching for volunteers.

Beside me, Delores shoots her hand up, drawing attention to our section.

Agnus and Bea also raise their hands, yelling, "Yoo-hoo!"

Wishing to turn invisible, I slink down in my seat.

Two young cowboys walk toward us. I lean away from Delores, Agnus, and Bea, trying to distance myself. *Do not make eye contact.*

Delores grabs my arm. Before I can protest, I'm ushered to the stage. Agnus and Bea bound eagerly behind us, once again foiling my escape. We climb the stairs. One of the dancers layers a Velcro saloon-girl costume over my clothes. She plops a bright-purple feathered headband onto my head. Then she places me in line with the other women, all of us facing the audience. The piano man begins playing fast. Delores loops her arm through mine on one side, and the cancan girl who dressed me loops her arm through my other one. I'm trapped.

The audience claps to the beat of the music. Heat rises from my toes to my face. My eyes grow big. I wonder if I look like a deer in headlights. I want to bolt but can't, linked to Delores on my left and the cancan girl on my right. The ladies on stage move with the music. The line shifts to the left, but I go right, bumping into the cancan girl. The line moves right, and I go left, bumping into Delores. She laughs, nonplussed at my clumsiness. I'm being pulled from both sides like a rope in a tug-of-war contest. Deciding I need to get in step with the line, I glance over at Delores. I'm momentarily transfixed by the happiness radiating from her. I peer past her. Agnus and Bea smile and laugh with each kick. The audience fades as I watch them. My troubles disappear. Feeling carefree, I kick, twirl, and laugh.

Delores glances my way and winks.

The music ends too soon. We are ushered off the stage. My face is hot and I'm out of breath, but my body tingles from the exhilarating experience. Through the remainder of the show, I steal side glances at Agnus, Bea, and Delores. They clap their hands to the beat of the music and giggle with each other. I'm more entertained watching them than the actual show. Delores catches me staring.

"Are you having fun?" Her sky-blue eyes sparkle under the bright lights.

"Yes," I say loud enough for her to hear me over the music.

She grins, then turns her attention back toward the stage.

This is the most fun I've had in a very long time.

# CHAPTER ELEVEN

O nce we return to our motel room, Bea says, "Let's play Truth or Dare."

Agnus groans. "Aren't we a little old for that game?"

Looking at the grandmotherly pajama-clad ladies, I cup my hand over my mouth to muffle a laugh.

"This is like a slumber party. You do remember those from when you were a girl?" Bea's tone drips with sarcasm as she raises an eyebrow.

Agnus rolls her eyes but doesn't comment.

"I want to go first." Delores removes the numerous bangles from her wrists and sets them on a nearby nightstand.

"Oh good! Thanks for playing along." Bea claps her hands, then glares at Agnus. "Go ahead."

Delores turns to me. "Sarah, truth or dare?" Her blue eyes bore into mine.

"I don't want to go first." I gulp. I hadn't expected to be a part of their game.

"I'll go easy on you." Her faded crimson lips form a teasing smile. "For now."

Sitting with my back resting against the headboard, I pull my knees to the center of my chest and wrap my arms around my shins.

All three ladies stare at me as if waiting me out.

Wincing, I concede. "Okay, truth."

Delores claps her hands with enthusiasm. She places a bejeweled finger under her chin, tilting her head sideways. "Hmm ... If you could travel anywhere, where would you go?"

I exhale a sigh of relief. Thankful for an easy question, I say, "Italy."

"Yes." Agnus gives me a high five. "On my bucket list too."

"Okay, now it's your turn, Sarah," says Delores.

I unwrap my arms from my knees and stretch my legs out on the bed. "Truth or dare?" I ask Agnus.

"I'm too old for silly dares, so truth."

"If you could meet any celebrity, who would it—"

"Colin Firth!" Agnus's answer bursts out like she knew the question before I asked it.

Delores and Bea belt out laughing.

"Hubba-hubba." Bea smiles and rubs her hands together.

We all giggle.

"Have you watched the BBC version of *Pride and Prejudice*?" Delores asks me.

"Yes, I have, but it's been a while."

"Agnus owns the DVD. We love to fast forward through the episodes to the scenes with Mr. Darcy." Delores clutches her stomach after another big belly laugh.

"Especially the swoon-worthy look he gives Elizabeth when she stands at the piano, turning each sheet of music for his little sister." Bea chuckles.

Agnus's face turns red, but she doesn't disagree.

Giggling, I say, "I'll have to rent it again and refresh my memory.

Bea's face grows serious. "Oh, no, don't do that. We have Jane Austin marathons all the time at Agnus's house. You'll have to join us."

Delores and Agnus both nod.

Warmed by the invitation, I smile. "I would love that."

My phone rings. "Excuse me while I check to see who's calling me." Once I dig my cell from my purse, I read the lit screen. *Emma.* I don't want to interrupt the game, so I say, "I'll be right back" and walk out into the motel corridor.

"Hi, Emma." I'm excited that *she* called me.

When I click "speaker," her voice echoes in the hallway. "Where have you been, Mom? I've been calling you for hours." She sounds cross.

I scan the hallway for anyone who might overhear our conversation. I'm all alone.

"Why?" My tone changes from excitement to concern. "Is everything okay?"

"Yes, Mom." Her tone is sharp. "I was calling to *check in* as you instructed. We are in Arizona."

I ignore her sarcasm. "Oh, sorry, honey. I turned off my phone while I was cancan dancing."

"You were what?" she asks.

Laughter explodes on the other side of our motel room door. FOMO—a funny term Emma taught me a few years ago —has me wanting to rejoin my friends. "Can I call you back later? The girls and I are playing Truth or Dare."

"We must have a bad connection, because I can't make sense of anything you're saying. And who is laughing in the background?" Emma's annoyance travels through the line loud and clear.

"My friends." Warmth fills my heart at those words. "I'll tell you about them when I call you back."

Emma says a flat, "Okay."

77

"Love you."

She hangs up without another word.

I stare at the screensaver on my phone—a family photo from a few years back. I trace Dave's and Emma's faces with my finger, exhaling a heavy sigh. Before I get all mopey, another burst of laughter pulls me back into our room.

"Everything all right?" Agnus asks when I sit on the bed.

"That was my daughter, Emma, checking in." I avert my gaze from making direct eye contact.

"Do you have a picture of her on your phone?" Delores asks.

I laugh because I have an absurd number of pictures of her. Already piled onto one bed, the women scrunch around me. I scroll through my digital tribute to Emma—baby pictures, soccer photos, birthday parties, and vacations—virtually Emma's whole life on display. I'm embarrassed by how long it takes to go through the photos. They must be so bored, but all three of them take a turn holding the phone and commenting on each picture, seeming genuinely interested.

Agnus hands the cell back to me after looking at the last photo. "She's beautiful." Her warm brown eyes study me over her horn-rimmed glasses.

My center warms and becomes gooey like a pastry straight out of the oven. "Thank you." My smile is bittersweet. Hearing Emma's voice tonight and going through her pictures only makes me miss her more.

Agnus's brows draw together. "What's wrong, Sarah?"

I'm embarrassed my facial expressions betrayed me. "I miss her. Our relationship has been a little strained the last few years."

They sit in silence, waiting for me to elaborate. Sharing my feelings has always been foreign to me. But as I look at each lady's face, warm and caring eyes meet mine.

Inhaling deeply, I begin. "I've struggled since Emma left for college. I know I should have developed a hobby or two, maybe found a job once she started school, but I loved being a stay-at-home mom. I did the proverbial 'put all my eggs in one basket.' My world has always revolved around Emma—my identity tied up in being a good mom." I hesitate, but Agnus's encouraging smile persuades me to continue.

"As Emma grew older, she started resenting my involvement in her life. She got frustrated whenever I joined the PTA, the school dance committee, or the Athletic Booster Club. I had been a room mom throughout her elementary years, so it seemed natural to be involved with whatever organizations supported her interests in middle and high school. I reasoned her frustration was teenage angst." I take another deep breath, gauging their expressions, wishing I knew what they were thinking. Do they find me pitiful? Feel sorry for me?

"Emma became even more distant when she started college. She ignored my calls and texts. Her visits home became less frequent. Sometimes I wouldn't hear from her for a month." The empty space in the pit in my stomach aches. My vision blurs.

Delores hands me a Kleenex.

"The night I met you all at the diner, Emma had come home for the first time in a long while. She and her boyfriend, Philip, got engaged last Christmas. The wedding date was set for next summer, a year from now. We were supposed to spend this summer working on their wedding plans. While I was excited about their upcoming nuptials, I was overjoyed to have my girl back home. I had made so many plans, but when Emma came home that night, she told me they had eloped. As if I wasn't already upset, she added another bombshell. They moved to Arizona this week." My chin trembles. I bow my head and stare at the tissue on my lap. I can't bear to see their faces. Maybe they are asking the same question I've asked myself multiple times. If I am a good mother, why is this happening?

"It's plain and simple." Bea's voice breaks into my painful chain of thoughts. "Kids can suck sometimes."

I force myself to lift my head.

"They have the ability to break your heart," adds Delores, and Bea nods in agreement. Delores's melancholy tone surprises me. Her fun personality and infectious laugh are absent. The silence that follows her statement is deafening.

After a moment, Agnus says, "Well, I like my kids."

Delores and Bea groan.

"What?" She shrugs. "I do. Not that they can't be a pain sometimes, but I like them. So sue me." She sticks her tongue out at the other two.

Turning to me, she says, "Sarah, give yourself some grace. Emma too. I'm sure you were and are a wonderful mom. It's a new chapter in both of your lives. Emma's a newly married woman, and you're beginning your third act."

"Third act?" I have no idea what she means.

Bea rises from the bed and stands, capturing our attention. "Please allow Professor Bea to explain." She takes a bow, then points an imaginary stick into the air.

"Oh, this should be good." Agnus shakes her head, then face-palms.

Bea ignores her. "The first act is your childhood," she says in a slow, dramatic, teacher-like voice. "The second act is marriage, then raising healthy and happy kids." She laughs, placing her right hand to the side of her mouth. "And hoping they don't turn into idiots when they're adults."

Delores and Agnus snort. I laugh, appreciating the release of some of the pent-up sadness.

"Each act is hard and has its own challenges. The third act

can be difficult to navigate, but ..." Bea pauses. "It can also be rewarding." She winks. "In the third act, your kids are out of the house, hopefully, and it's back to being only you and your spouse."

Delores's face drains of color.

Bea stops, and her eyes squeeze tight. She clears her throat, then bends to place a soft kiss on Delores's cheek. "Sorry, my friend. I wasn't thinking," she whispers.

Delores's eyes grow misty. "It's okay." She squeezes Bea's hand.

After a few moments, Delores is poised again and clarifies, "I think what Bea means to say is the third act can be spent doing the things you didn't have the time, energy, or resources to accomplish when you were younger. You need to ask yourself: With all the wisdom and experience you now have in your arsenal, how will you use the time you have left?"

Sweat pops out on the back of my neck. Her pale-blue eyes seem to pierce my innermost thoughts. She leans in closer. "What dreams or goals have you left unfinished? Who do you want to be in this last stage of your life, Sarah?"

I give her my honest response. "I have no idea."

# CHAPTER TWELVE

Deciding we've had enough *truth* for one night, we only do dares. The game concludes at 2 A.M. We all lie down in our beds—lights out, no more talking.

My stomach muscles ache from laughing at the silly things Delores and Bea dared us to do. I smile at the soft snores in the bed across from me. Delores, probably too tired to toss and turn tonight, remains still beside me. Too wound up to sleep, I lay staring at the ceiling as the day's events replay. I smile and file the memories away. Unexpectedly, my thoughts dial back three years to the day we dropped Emma off at college.

\* \* \*

The heat index is one hundred degrees when we pull our vehicle into the dorm lot. Numerous cars and minivans shuffle in and out of parking spaces after the occupants unload a dorm-full of contents for their promising college students.

Sighing, I open my door. A blast of heat hits me. Dave and Emma stand outside the car, stretching their backs and legs after the long drive. Not wanting to start the day crying, I kept busy packing up the van this morning, averting my eyes from Emma. But now I take a good long look at her. Her ebony hair is tied into a messy topknot. She's wearing the new burgundy college tee we purchased the day of her initial college tour, distressed denim shorts, and a pair of white high-top tennis shoes. Blinking back hot tears, I pull out boxes to set on a cart provided by the school.

Streams of sweat pour down my neck as I carry the boxes up the stairs to the third floor. Once inside her home away from home, I clean and sanitize the concrete hospital-white-walled dorm room while Dave sets up her electronics. I can tell Emma is nervous by the way she chews on her lower lip while unpacking her items in the small space. The school she picked is not close. Coming home often will be impractical.

Not wanting her to feel anxious or sad, I say, "College is going to be great. You're going to make so many new friends."

She nods and continues to hang up her clothes, avoiding eye contact. The tears I've been holding back have my head pounding as they beg for release. "You'll be home all the time. It'll be like you never left."

Emma's lips form a tight smile. Her eyes lift to meet mine, then she crosses over in a rush to hug me. Her wet face touches mine. Tears trickle from my own eyes now too.

"I could use a little help over here." Dave breaks the moment.

We separate, wiping our faces with the backs of our hands. Emma walks over to help Dave set up her computer while I busy myself making her bed.

It doesn't take long to set up her room. I keep trying to find things to do to prolong leaving her. Dave keeps reminding me we have a long drive back.

Sighing, I give her one more hug. Dave and I walk into the

hallway. Before Emma shuts the door, I say, "We'll see you Labor Day weekend," trying to sound positive, but my voice cracks.

Fatigue sets in with every step I take farther from Emma. Once outside, Dave takes my hand, walking me to the passenger side. He opens my door, but I hesitate.

He gives me a stern look. "She'll be okay."

I force myself to climb in, then Dave closes the door. I think he's afraid I'll make a mad dash back to Emma. He gets in on his side, pats my leg, and gives me a sympathetic smile. His kind gesture has my eyes stinging and nose burning again. I reach behind me to grab a box of tissues. My throat catches. Emma's seat is empty.

Flashbacks of her sitting in *that seat* for so many years swirl through my memory—telling us about her day at school or repeating something funny one of her friends said in class. Emma excited about a new movie coming out and making me promise to take her to the theater as soon as it premiered. Driving carpool for her and her soccer teammates, listening to them giggle while talking about the cute new boy at school. Emma and I singing at the top of our lungs to one of the newest boy-band songs.

Poor Dave. I cry all the way home. He looks wretched, white-knuckling the steering wheel until we reach our driveway.

\* \* \*

Four alarms go off. When did I fall asleep, and why is my pillow wet? Wiping my eyes, I watch Delores, Bea, and Agnus rise from their beds. We're turning into a well-oiled machine with our morning routine. Each of us knows when it's our turn to shower and use the vanity. Being an only child, I wonder if this is what it's like having sisters.

In under an hour, we are out the door. We sound like a gaggle of geese as we head next door to a local café for breakfast. In the parking lot, our bouts of laughter in between stories turn heads our way. Feeling happier than I have in a while, I practically float into the café. We find a booth while rehashing yesterday's events.

"Sarah, you be the judge. Who did you think had the highest kick in our cancan dance last night?" Bea points her thumbs at her chest.

"It was me." Delores pumps her hands in the air. Her bracelets clap like applause.

"Was not," argues Agnus. "We all know I had the highest kicks. Plus, I was in step with the saloon girls. Humph."

I place my hand under my chin in a thinking pose. "Hmm." With a sly smile, I say, "It was me."

They all give me an eye roll. "Really, Sarah?" Delores says.

Bea bluntly asks, "Didn't you accidently kick one of the saloon girls because you went the wrong way?"

Delores gasps. Agnus studies the tabletop. Do they think Bea offended me?

She doesn't back down. Instead, she stares pointedly at me, waiting for my rebuttal.

I cackle until an unexpected snort escapes my nose.

Delores joins me with a big belly laugh. Agnus and Bea both chuckle.

"You should have seen that young girl's face when I kicked her," I say. "She was not happy. She tried to trade places with the girl next to her, but the other girl kept shaking her head." Another stream of giggles escapes me. The stitch in my side makes me hold my stomach.

"I wondered what was going on," Delores says between

giggles. "Agnus was pulling me one way, and you were pulling me the other. All the while, Bea was kicking her little heart out."

We explode again, howling at the mental image.

Bea blushes, then chortles. "Well, the show must go on, regardless of whether there are legs flying everywhere." Our laughter fills the diner.

When the waitress approaches our table, we haven't even opened our menus. She taps her notepad while we scan the breakfast options.

With her eyes boring down on us, I ask, "Do you have any pie?"

She points to a whiteboard on the wall behind her, where an assortment of homemade pies is listed.

"I'll take a pecan pie and a cup of black coffee," I say.

"We'll take the same," Delores, Agnus, and Bea chime in together.

Once the waitress returns with our orders, we clink our coffee cups together.

Bea shouts, "Pie to celebrate the greatest cancan dancers this side of the Mississippi River."

# CHAPTER THIRTEEN

W hen we board the bus, we switch seats with the ladies who usually sit behind Agnus and Bea so it's easier to visit with each other during the ride to Manitou Springs, Colorado.

Bob stands holding his clipboard at the front, silently marking off our names. He's matched our faces with the names on the list, so we no longer have to raise our hands. With his last checkmark, he nods at Frank. The bus jerks forward and knocks us back into our seats.

"Whoa," several women yell.

My carry-on falls out of the overhead compartment to the floor. As I retrieve it, I witness several others doing the same.

"Sorry about that." Frank glances at us in the big rearview mirror. He continues to push the accelerator, bouncing us onto the interstate on-ramp. He gives Bob an uncertain look, then as the bus smooths out and gains speed, he shrugs.

Bob shrugs back.

Everyone has retrieved their items and once again taken their seats. Agnus and Bea twist around so we can visit. After our game of Truth or Dare, they know more about me than I do them.

"Agnus, tell me more about your family. How many kids do you have?" I'm confused when Bea rolls her eyes and laughs.

"I have eight kids." She nudges Bea with her elbow. "Four girls and four boys."

"Eight?" I swallow hard. "Wow. I can't imagine taking care of so many kids."

"She does it like a boss." Delores smiles at Agnus.

"I'm only giving her a hard time about having so many children. She doesn't take any nonsense from them," Bea says. "They were the best-behaved kids growing up and have become wonderful adults. They respect their momma, that's for sure." She gives a thumbs-up.

Agnus blushes, then smiles. "Now, Bea, you always act like my family is perfect." She turns to me. "We have our flaws."

Bea laughs. "If you look up the word 'matriarch' in the dictionary, you'll find a picture of Agnus beside it. They're the closest bunch of people you'll ever meet. I'm surprised they've lasted this long without their momma."

"Oh, Bea." Agnus huffs and rolls her eyes. "Don't be so dramatic."

"How do you do it?" I think about the distance between Emma and me.

"A lot of prayers," Agnus says.

"Did you have trouble missing them a lot when they all left home?" I ask.

"How could she?" Bea snorts. "They all live within a five-mile radius of her house. They spend more time there than at their own homes. We were astounded when Agnus agreed to this trip, traveling so far away from her family."

"In all fairness, Bea, we're always welcomed by her family

when we go to her house. You're sounding a little put out," Delores scolds.

Bea shrugs. "Maybe so." She crosses her arms across her chest and purses her lips. An awkward silence hangs between us.

Is Bea jealous of Agnus's close-knit family? Or maybe she doesn't like sharing her friend.

"How many kids do you have, Bea?" I shift the attention away from Agnus.

Bea's lively eyes cloud over. "Two," she says in a flat voice.

Delores and Agnus study their hands. Bea doesn't offer anything more. Her pained expression tells me her kids are a sore subject, so I refrain from asking for details.

The bus pulls over and slows to a stop on the shoulder of the road.

Bob rises from his seat. The boom of the microphone coming to life has many of us covering our ears. He turns a knob to lower the volume, then says, "We're going to take a group picture."

Grateful for some time to stretch our legs, we pile off the bus in single file.

Bob directs us into position as we group together in front of the Welcome to Colorful Colorado sign. Bob hands his cell over to Frank, then joins us.

Frank snaps several photos, checks them, then gives a thumbs-up.

Bob doesn't seem to be in a hurry to get us back on the bus, so I use this opportunity to walk past the sign and onto the grassy terrain. It may be my imagination, but as I breathe in deeply, the air seems cleaner and crisper. Snow-capped mountains tower in the distance. Colorful wildflowers blanket the hills and valleys all around me. I snap some pictures with my cell, then send them to Emma and Dave with the word

"*Beautiful.*" I'm not sure if they'll reply, but I'm not wasting this moment wondering. Instead of waiting for the three dots to appear, I tuck my phone into my back pocket.

"Time to go," Bob yells so all of us who wandered from the bus can hear him.

I stroll back, not wanting to leave such a beautiful place only to be confined once again in the stuffy blue tube. Only a few women haven't climbed back into the bus. I get in line behind Bea. She smiles at me, but it doesn't reach her eyes. I regret asking about her family. Her reaction to my question creates a dull ache in my chest. My heart hurts for her, and I don't even know why.

Once seated, Bob nods to Frank.

When Frank puts the bus into gear, a horrible groaning fills the air, and the entire frame begins to vibrate. Leaning to peer down the aisle, I witness Bob and Frank exchange worried glances. The bus grinds and rattles, then the jerking reluctantly subsides as we pick up speed on the highway. The women, usually talking and laughing, are dead quiet.

Bob turns his back to us and raises his cell to his ear. His hair moves with each nod and shake of his head. He holds the cell with his left hand while flailing his right arm as he talks to the person on the other end.

Bob gives a final nod, then puts his cell down. He shifts toward us, once again lifting the silver microphone. "Ladies, I hope you're okay with not stopping for lunch." His voice sinks.

An outpouring of groans fills the bus.

"I know, I know." He holds his free palm in a stop position reminiscent of a school crossing guard holding back traffic. Once everyone is quiet again, he explains, "Our bus seems to be having some engine problems, so we need to go straight to Manitou. There's a mechanic there who can look at it."

"How much farther do we have?" someone yells from the back.

"About three hours," Bob says.

More loud groans fill the air.

His jaw tenses, and his left eye twitches. He stares at us for a long moment. "I'm really sorry, but if we stop now, we might not get the bus going again." His tone is low and slow as if he's talking to a bunch of children. No one says a word. "If you don't have any travel snacks or drinks, there's bottled water in the back, and I have some snacks I can share." After rustling through his backpack, he holds up a half-eaten bag of Cool Ranch Doritos and three red-licorice sticks.

Thirty-some ladies erupt into loud laughter.

His face grows crimson. He spins around without another word, plops into his seat, and throws his snacks into his backpack.

Popping and crinkling sound from all directions. A smorgasbord of junk food passes back and forth, up and down the aisles, ensuring everyone has something to eat. We munch and crunch until we reach our motel in Manitou. With bloated bellies and tummy aches, we exit the bus and carry our luggage to our next home away from home.

# CHAPTER FOURTEEN

**M**anitou Springs is quaint, with a reputation of good food and unique gift shops. Our motel is conveniently located near the center of town. After we check in, the motel clerk hands us a map. Triangles highlight each natural spring fountain around the square. When we step outside, several other tourists crowd the sidewalks. Pikes Peak stands in the distance—it's snow-covered top gleaming under the sunshine —magnificent and picturesque.

We walk until we reach the first fountain on the map.

"What does this one taste like, I wonder?" Bea cups her hand under the water, then lowers her head to throw back a big gulp. She sputters, splattering water down the front of her tee, and scrunches her nose. "Blech." She wipes her mouth with the back of her hand.

Curious, I cup my hand and let the cold water fill it. I lick the water like a cat, not wanting a mouthful like Bea. A putrid smell fills my nostrils. The water tastes similar to what I imagine a rotten egg would taste like. The strong pungent aftertaste lingers on my tongue. I fling the rest of the water on the ground, then retrieve a small bottle of hand sanitizer to rub into my palms.

Delores wrinkles her nose. "I'll pass."

"Me too." Agnus shakes her head slowly. "Are we sure it's safe to drink? Doesn't look very sanitary."

Eying the green residue on the basin of the fountain, I have to admit she makes a good point.

We continue down the sidewalk until we find another well.

"It says the mineral spring water has medicinal purposes and can heal many ailments." Delores reads aloud from the map. "I wonder if it could heal my arthritis." She grins. "It also says this well is sweet and has been used to make the town's lemonade." She cups her hands under the fountain, and the water seeps between her closed fingers as she sticks her tongue in her palm. "Not too bad."

Agnus goes next. "Here's to healing my sciatic-nerve pain." She cups her hands under the fountain and gulps the water down before it can escape through the cracks between her fingers.

Bea copies Agnus, smiling after drinking the cool water. "The water is sweet. Here's to being young again."

"Wrong fountain," Delores says. "We need a trip to Florida for that one."

We all laugh.

"Okay, it's your turn, Sarah," Bea says. "What do you need healed?"

The stream of cool fresh water makes my palms tingle when I place them in the fountain. I want a redo—to fix whatever caused this chasm between Emma and me. But like Delores said, this isn't the fountain of youth. It's also not a time machine or wishing well. Trying to think of my least revealing wish, I say, "Straight, glossy hair. I'm tired of trying to fix my curly, frizzy mess." I laugh, lifting a section of hair.

"Hats work great for me." Bea touches the bill of her orange baseball cap, which matches today's athletic jacket and pants.

"You may be onto something. That may be my next purchase," I say.

"You're beautiful either way. Let your hair hang down any way you like. You're with friends," Delores says, not a hair out of place in her chic cropped bob. Even though everything about her seems perfect, her warm smile encourages me to believe her compliment is genuine.

Done taste testing spring water, we check out several of the shops and small art galleries. Taking my time perusing without Dave's and Emma's voices in the background impatiently saying, "Aren't you ready to go yet?" is wonderful.

We all chatter back and forth, showing each other interesting and unusual items we find along the way. Once we've finished shopping in a cute little whimsical store, we walk back outside.

"We need a selfie with Pikes Peak in the background," Bea says.

We cluster together. Bea stretches her arm out as far as she can reach, trying to get all of us in the frame with Pikes Peak in the background. After each click, she brings the phone closer to our faces. Each picture is worse than the one before. She's documented a collage of eyes and noses. Bouts of giggles rise with each attempt.

"You can see my double chin," Agnus hollers.

"My eyes are closed," Bea complains.

"You were taking a power nap." Delores laughs. "I'm not sure what I was looking at." In the last photo, she's looking off to the side.

"Do you want me to take your photo?" a man nearby asks.

"Yes, that would be wonderful." Bea hands him her cell,

then takes the few steps back to us and places her arm around Agnus's shoulders.

Agnus extends her arm around Delores's shoulders, and Delores pulls me closer, wrapping her arm around my shoulders. Warmth spreads across my face, travels down my neck, and settles in my heart. I smile at my newfound friends. The man snaps the picture.

"Are you ladies sisters?" he asks.

We giggle.

"We are the sisters we chose for ourselves." Delores may have stolen that saying from a coffee mug in one of the gift shops.

The man laughs and hands the cell back to Bea. "Enjoy your day," he says before walking away.

"What a weird question." Bea shakes her head. "We couldn't look or be more different from one another."

"We're sisters from another mother and father," Delores titters. "And now we have a little sister." She glances at me.

My heart overflows with a sense of belonging and something more. What? How do I name the unfamiliar feeling?

My phone dings with a notification. I open the text from Bea and find our recent picture. While my friends discuss what to do next, I study the photo. The mountain behind us is captivating, but the joyful expressions on each of our faces— Priceless.

I text the picture to Dave and Emma and add:

> Manitou Springs is amazing. Wish you were here.

Dave returns only a thumbs-up emoji. He's obviously still mad. Emma doesn't respond at all. I'm sure she's busy and will text later, I reason, not wanting to spoil this happy moment.

"Sarah and I need another charm for our bracelets." Delores points to a souvenir shop farther down the sidewalk.

"I will meet you at the restaurant across the street," Agnus says. "I wore the wrong shoes for all this walking. I'm getting a blister on my ankle." She points to the brown sandals on her feet.

"I'll go with you." Bea nods, then they leave together.

Delores and I stroll to another quaint shop. Upon entering, streaks of colored light from the stained-glass windows flood the wooden floors. It takes me a moment to step out of the doorway as I savor the scent of lavender filling the air. Delores makes a beeline for a large wooden display cabinet near the register. LED lights illuminate the jewelry under the locked glass top.

Beside the twinkling Swarovski crystals lies a large assortment of charms.

Delores bends to get a closer view, moving her eyeglasses up and down with her right hand. "Which charm should we pick, Sarah?"

"Can I ask you a question, Delores?" My tone is meek.

"Of course. Anything." She doesn't glance up. "Except how old I am."

"No, never." I chuckle, then my tone turns serious. "I was wondering why Bea got upset when I mentioned her kids."

Delores pauses from her perusal and swivels toward me. Her eyebrows draw together. She opens her mouth but closes it again.

I wince. "I'm sorry. It's none of my business. I shouldn't have asked. It's just the memory of Bea's stricken face has me feeling awful for bringing up what must be a painful subject."

Delores glances around. The shop is empty except for the elderly man at the cash register. He's been reading a newspaper the whole time we've been here, never looking up —not even when we entered the shop.

She hesitates. "You have to promise not to say a word. *Okay?*" she whispers.

I nod, uncertain whether I've opened Pandora's box.

"Bea's had a rough time of it," Delores says. "I tell her to give it time, but she is so hurt. Agnus, Irene, and I pray for her every day, hoping the situation will get better." She pauses, sighs, then explains, "Bea and Pete, her husband, had—or have —two kids, depending on how you look at it. Fraternal twins. Theodore is named after Pete's dad, but we all call him Teddy. Their daughter, Millie, is named after Bea's favorite aunt."

Delores scans the store again. "Let's move over there." She points to an old wooden table with two chairs near the front window.

I nod, then follow her.

Once we take our seats, she continues, "Bea, Agnus, Irene, and I all went to school together. We have been friends since kindergarten. Our kids grew up together." Delores smiles, then her lips purse into a frown. "I digress." She wrings her hands. "When Millie was seventeen, she was killed in a car wreck."

I gasp. "Oh, no." My stomach tightens. Losing a child is a parent's worst nightmare.

"There's more." Delores glances at the ceiling, then down again at me. "Teddy was driving. They were headed to their junior prom."

My heart sinks. I'm sick for my new friend.

The corners of Delores's eyes fill with tears. "Bea and Pete never blamed Teddy for the accident. He was a responsible teen and a good driver. A terrible downpour came unexpectedly. The car hydroplaned, and Teddy lost control. Millie was declared dead at the scene. Teddy was banged up with broken ribs, a concussion, and internal bleeding. For many days, it was touch and go for him. Our community held prayer vigils for the family in the parking lot of the hospital. Once Teddy's mind cleared, he started asking about Millie. Bea didn't tell him she was gone until he was out of intensive care. The news crushed him."

Delores chokes up from the stream of tears running down her face.

"I'm so sorry that happened to Bea and her family." I can't imagine how I would survive if I lost Emma. Could I even come back from that? I have a new respect for Bea. The strength she must have, bearing something so heartbreaking.

Delores takes a tissue from her purse and wipes under her eyes. "There's more."

"How can there be more?"

She slumps in her chair. Her usually bright eyes are dull and sad. "Once Teddy came home, he couldn't forgive himself." Her voice cracks. "No matter how hard Bea and Pete tried to convince him it wasn't his fault, Teddy wouldn't listen. Fast forward a year, and he is a senior in high school. A new girl enrolls—Samantha."

Delores pauses. "Samantha is ..." She puts her hand to her lips, then moves it to the side of her mouth. "... very controlling and manipulative. She fueled Teddy's anger and grief, making up horrible lies about Bea and Pete." Her voice is so quiet, I have to lean closer to hear everything. "She twisted their words and actions, making Teddy believe they blamed him for his sister's death. Samantha even went so far as to tell him she overheard them say they wished he would have died instead of Millie." She pounds the table with her fist. "An absolute lie. Bea tried to make Teddy understand that Samantha was no good for him, but the more she tried to persuade him, the more Samantha pushed. He moved out after graduation. A month later, he secretly married Samantha."

I shake my head in disbelief. "What a sad situation" are the only words I come up with.

Delores nods. "Teddy and Samantha live ten miles from his parents, but Bea and Pete aren't allowed to visit. Teddy won't come home either. One day, while Bea was shopping at the grocery store, one of Teddy's neighbors asked about Bea's granddaughter. That's how she found out about the baby." Delores exhales a long breath and wipes away fresh tears. "Her name is Millie."

# CHAPTER FIFTEEN

Delores and I cross the street to rejoin Bea and Agnus for dinner. All four of us are unusually quiet after ordering our meals. No one seems to have anything to talk about, so we eat in silence. After finishing my food, I take out my compact and check my appearance. Dark circles and puffiness linger beneath my eyes.

Agnus suggests we turn in early. We all agree. The others look as tired as I feel. We make our way back to our motel, unpack our bags, and settle in for the night.

I sit on the bed, watching Bea on the other side of the room as she sets the alarm on her phone. I want to hug her, but she would wonder why. I can't break Delores's trust.

Bea catches me staring and shoots me a questioning look. I shift my gaze to my purse on my lap. Digging with no purpose, I pull my cell phone out and stare at the blank screen. After a few moments, I peek at Bea again.

She seems to have forgotten me.

Once everyone is in bed, I text Dave and Emma good night.

I roll to my side and face the wall, not wanting the glow of my phone to keep Delores awake as I wait for a response.

Dave texts me a sleepy-face emoji. Maybe he's cooling down? I can hope. I wait several more minutes for Emma to reply, but she doesn't. A dull stab hits my heart—the same one I feel every time she ignores me.

I shut my eyes tight, praying for a deep, forgetful sleep. Instead, images of my little girl swirl through my dreams. She sits on my lap, dressed in her pink ballet costume. The oversized pink bow used to tie her hair up in a ponytail shakes when she bounces. The netting from her layered skirt flutters around us while she embraces my neck with her small soft arms.

"How much do you love me?" Her sweet voice is playful. She giggles, loving this game.

I spread my thumb and index finger on my right hand an inch. "This much?"

Emma giggles again, shaking her head.

I take both of my hands and place them a few inches from each other. "This much?" I ask.

Emma laughs and shakes her head again. She holds my hands with her small dimpled ones and stretches them as far from each other as her little arms can reach.

"Oh, this much," I tease and wink at her.

Delores mumbles something in her sleep, waking me from my dream. She's draped her arm over my shoulder. Carefully, I remove her arm and slide closer to the edge of the bed. I close my eyes, longing to reenter the dream, but it's gone.

# CHAPTER SIXTEEN

**M**orning arrives, and before long, we are dressed and ready for today's adventure. We make our way to the motel lobby for breakfast.

Bob follows us. "I have an announcement to make," he yells over the visiting and eating crowd. "Unfortunately, the bus is still in the shop. The mechanic's waiting on some parts. He is hopeful it will be fixed tomorrow."

A chorus of complaints fills the lobby.

Bob holds his hands up until the murmurs cease. "I know. I know. It's disappointing. I thought we would be on the road this morning. Unfortunately, that's not the case."

A group of women rush toward him, silencing his apologies and explanations with their complaints.

"Well, that stinks," Bea states flatly. "What are we supposed to do in Manitou Springs for another day?" She drops her gaze to her cup of coffee.

"We can walk around the town again," offers Agnus. When none of us responds, she suggests, "Or pull out the card games we brought."

Bea grunts, stirring her coffee in continuous circles.

"I was looking forward to going to the Garden of the Gods," Delores says dejectedly.

We all nod in agreement.

I pull out the Garden of the Gods brochure I stuffed in my purse when we checked in. "Maybe they have a shuttle?"

Agnus, Bea, and Delores give me hopeful looks as I scan the brochure.

"I don't see any mention of it." I frown, plopping it on the table.

After a beat, Bea's face lights up. "What about those people who will come and get you? Goober, I think."

"Do you mean Uber?" Agnus laughs.

"Uber, goober, they sound the same," Bea says gruffly.

"I've never taken an Uber." Worry lines crinkle Delores's brow. "Have you, Sarah?"

"I haven't, but Emma takes them all the time. It's scary to me to get in a car with a stranger, but she thinks it's fine." I bite my lower lip. "I guess it's no different than a taxi."

Bea perks up. She stops stirring her coffee and stares at me. Is she waiting for me to make the call?

I exhale a loud breath, then roll up my sleeves. "I think we need an app for it." I grab my phone from my purse. "Let me call Emma. She'll know how to do it."

They cheer, then watch as I tap Emma's number.

The call goes straight to her voicemail.

My face flushes from embarrassment and, I have to admit, a little anger. But I say in a sweet, soft tone, "This is your mom. Can you call me back?"

Agnus, Bea, and Delores have taken over the brochure, excitedly planning what we will do with our day.

I claim my phone only has one bar and excuse myself to go outside. Stalling, I pray Emma will call me back. Several minutes pass. I'm sure she's busy—not ignoring me. But her track record speaks for itself. She's not going to call me back. I'll try to figure out the process myself.

My chest tightens as I download the Uber app. Technology always makes me nervous. I read and reread the directions on the web browser. Semi-satisfied I have figured the app out, I walk back into the breakfast area. When I reach our table, everyone looks at me with hopeful anticipation on their faces.

"It shows only one Uber available that can seat four passengers. Do you want me to request it?"

With big smiles, they nod.

I tap on my phone to confirm the request. "Okay, our Uber is on its way," I beam. I didn't need help after all.

We huddle together over the small table, deep in planning, when Bob interrupts us. "Someone's asking for Sarah Goodwin." He points to the motel counter.

A tall young man visits with the motel clerk. He's dressed in a black-and-gold plaid shirt, jeans, and cowboy boots. A black baseball cap with "UCCS" embroidered in bold gold sits on his head.

"Wow, that was fast." I check my watch.

"It's our *Uber* coming for us." Delores raises one eyebrow at Bob.

He chuckles. "Well, you girls have fun."

Delores grins. "Oh, we will."

Bob's eyes crinkle, then he walks away. Is he amused?

We all rise from the table and cross over to meet our driver.

"Hello, ladies," he drawls, then flashes an endearing crooked smile. "I'm Sid." He extends his hand to each of us, giving friendly, firm handshakes all around. After introductions, he leads us outside. "There's my vehicle."

Our eyes follow the invisible line from the tip of his finger to a big red king-cab truck with an incredibly high lift. Blue lights glow beneath its frame.

Agnus's mouth gapes. Delores covers hers, muffling a giggle. Bea rolls her eyes.

I whisper so Sid can't hear me, "Maybe I can find us another ride." I don't want to insult the ladies, but they *are* all older than me. Will they even be able to get in the cab? I'm not sure I can.

Shifting my attention to Sid, I say, "Thank you for coming to get us, but I think we've changed our minds."

Agnus looks relieved.

"Don't be ridiculous. This ride works just fine." Delores nods and looks over at the three of us.

Agnus sighs and glances wide-eyed at Bea. "I'm game if you are."

She tilts her head toward the sky and groans. "I'm in, I guess."

Sid breaks out into a huge grin before he opens the back passenger door. There's no running board to step up on. Agnus stares at the floorboard of the truck.

"Here, let me help you," Sid offers. "I help my grandma get in all the time."

"Great," Agnus growls under her breath.

"First, grab the handle by the window with your right hand, then place your left foot on the floorboard," he instructs.

Agnus motions Bea closer. "Come here, Bea. You're always wanting to play games. How long has it been since you've played Twister?"

Bea doesn't laugh but moves next to her. Agnus stretches to reach the handle with her right hand while gripping Bea's shoulder with her left for balance.

"Now push off with your right leg," Sid says.

Agnus narrows her eyes. She grimaces, then shoves off. Sid's big hands grip her hips as he catapults her into the cab.

Agnus yelps as she flies onto the bench seat, her face plastered against the black upholstery. Clutching the vinyl, she lifts herself into a seated position and blinks slowly. She stares straight ahead as she slides across the bench to the other side.

Bea, Delores, and I cover our mouths to hold back our cackles.

Setting her jaw, Bea instructs Sid, "Cup your hands like this."

He makes a small basket with his hands by interweaving his fingers.

Bea places her right foot in the handbasket while pushing off his shoulder to jump into the cab. She kicks the back of his head with her left foot. His hat flies off, hitting the asphalt behind him. Bea lands on the bench seat. She gives Sid a curt nod and Agnus a cocky smile.

Sid takes a deep breath and picks up his UCCS hat from the ground. He places it on his head, then turns to Delores.

Next to the monster truck, she appears even smaller than usual.

Sid points to her high-wedge shoes. "I don't know that your friends' tactics will work for you with those on, ma'am."

"You're a big boy. Can't you just throw me in?" Delores asks.

Sid hesitates, then lifts her over his left shoulder like a sack of potatoes. He plops her in the seat, her top twisted and cockeyed. Her bangles clang. Delores adjusts her clothing and pats her hair down, then flashes a brilliant smile. Ever the beauty queen, even when jostled.

Sid shuts the door and opens mine. I get shotgun, though I never called it. Sid bends his left knee out and extends his right hand. I've seen this position used by some of Emma's cheerleader friends when they practiced their stunts in our backyard pool. They tried to persuade Emma to switch to cheerleading, but soccer had her heart.

I step on his knee with my right foot, holding his hand for balance. I jump to the floorboard with my left foot, grabbing the handle inside for dear life until I pull myself into the truck. Giddiness fills me. I made it.

Sid runs around to the driver's side, takes his seat, and starts the ignition. The truck gives a loud rumble.

"Did someone steal your catalytic converter?" Delores yells over the engine's roar.

Sid laughs as he shifts into drive.

I glance at our motel as we pull out. Bob stands in front of the entrance, and our eyes lock. He's covering his mouth with his clipboard while holding his stomach with his other hand. The crinkles around his eyes make it obvious he is laughing.

"Sid," Agnus yells from the back, "unless you have a fireman's net for us to jump into when we reach our destination, how do you propose to get us out of here? Not that getting in wasn't fun."

Bea and Delores giggle.

Sid's face turns crimson.

"I have an idea." I point to a Walmart ahead.

Sid pulls into the parking lot.

When he starts to open his door, I say, "I've got it." Putting on a show for Bob was one thing, but making a spectacle of myself in a crowded parking lot of people with video-recording cell phones? No thank you.

I grip the handle above the window with my left hand and hold tightly to my seat with the other. I hoist myself down until I'm close enough to drop to the pavement. "I'll be right back." I grab my purse from the floorboard.

Ten minutes later, I power walk to the truck, holding my purchase up like a trophy for Agnus, Bea, and Delores to see.

"Ta-da!" I shout.

Sid comes around to my side of the truck. After unfolding the brand-new stepladder, he extends his hand. I climb the steps with his support and take my seat.

"Pretty proud of yourself, huh, Sarah?" Delores chortles.

I twist to look at her. My lips spread into a smug smile. "Yes, I am."

Bea and Agnus clap. I take a seated bow.

# CHAPTER SEVENTEEN

The trip from our motel to the Garden of the Gods is short. Sid steers the truck into the visitor center. We dismount from the cab using the stepladder and Sid's shoulder for balance.

"So, how does this work?" Agnus turns to Sid. "Are you assigned to us now?"

He scrunches his brows together as he looks at her. Then his face clears. "Oh, I was confused for a second. If you want me to pick you up when you're done, here's my cell number. I'm not sure if I'm supposed to give this out, but I trust you ladies. I'll be back here in a jiffy. I'm a little homesick, so it would be nice to spend some more time with you all, even if it's only for a brief drive. Hanging out with you feels akin to hanging out with my grandma." He smiles his big crooked smile, exhibiting his boyish charm.

Agnus, Bea, and Delores seem to take the words as a compliment, but I'm a little put out. How old does he think I am? I'm too young to be his grandma.

"You can hang out with us all day if you like," Delores says.

"I wouldn't want to intrude." He darts his gaze at his boots.

"You can be our tour guide," Agnus chimes in.

Bea groans and rolls her eyes, and Agnus jabs her with an elbow.

Sid's head snaps up, and he's beaming like a kid in a candy shop with a pocketful of money. "If you're sure, I would love that."

Bea frowns. "We always seem to have an entourage everywhere we go," she whispers to me.

I purse my lips and nod, but in my heart, I hope she doesn't feel the same way about me.

Sid strolls into the visitor center to get a map of the park. While we wait on a bench outside, I check out our footwear. Bea, Agnus, and I are wearing tennis shoes. Pointing at Delores's four-inch wedges, I ask, "Will you be able to walk the trails in those?"

"Probably." She grins. "But I don't want to muss them up." Delores winks and pulls out a pair of tennis shoes from her bag. Rhinestones shimmer on the sides of the white leather. She ties the pink laces intertwined with glittery silver threads into a bow. "Better?" She smirks.

I chuckle and nod my approval.

Sid returns and informs us that we'll have to drive to the trailhead. Once again, we pile into his truck, and he drives down the highway.

"Thank you again, ladies, for allowing me to join you," Sid says with a wide grin. "I haven't been here yet, either."

"A lot of help he's going to be," Bea complains loud enough for all of us to hear.

The cab goes quiet. I fiddle with my hat strap, trying to think of something to say to fill the awkward silence.

Agnus leans forward. "Where are you from, Sid?"

"A small town in Texas. You've probably never heard of it."
His smile is wistful.

"How did you end up here?" Delores asks.

His face brightens. "I got a scholarship at UCCS. I just finished my freshman year." He pauses, then with a melancholy smile, he continues, "I'm grateful to the university for providing this wonderful opportunity, but I miss my family and our farm."

I wait a beat, feeling the heaviness of his last words. "What kind of farm does your family have? Crops, or cattle?"

Sid lifts his chin when he turns my direction. "Texas Longhorn cattle." He puffs out his chest.

A few minutes later, we reach our destination. After using the stepladder to exit the truck again, we walk to the first rock formation.

"This one is called the Tower of Babel." Agnes reads more information from the map in her hands.

We stand in a horizontal line, tilting our heads from one side to the other, taking pauses in between.

After a few moments of studying the formation, Bea states flatly, "I don't see it. It's just two tall, skinny rocks."

Delores snorts. "Whether you see it or not, it's beautiful in my opinion."

"I think it's beautiful too." I study the coral colors of sand and rock surrounding us.

I pull my cell out of my back pocket. Turning slowly in a circle, I snap pictures of the rock formations. Once I've made a full circle, I lower my phone and check the pictures. I grimace. The photos don't do the magnificent beauty justice. Why didn't I grab my good camera from home? Probably because I haven't used it in years. Flashes of memory transport me back to my college days—dipping paper with a long tong into developing solution, then watching shiny white pages transform into colorful images. I loved spending time in the darkroom.

The memory surprises me. I haven't thought about my journalism classes in years. I shake my head and return to the present.

We continue walking. The sun is high in the sky. It's warm, but I'm thankful for a cool breeze from the north. Agnus rubs sunscreen across her arms and face, then offers the tube to me. I dab some on my own arms and face. Thanks to Bea's advice, a wide-brimmed hat hides most of my face.

"Sid, would you take a picture of us in front of the Kissing Camels?" I ask.

"Of course." He extends his hand for my phone.

Agnus, Delores, and I position ourselves in front of the formation, but Bea doesn't join us.

"Come on, Bea. Sid's trying to take our picture," Agnus says.

She continues walking on the trail ahead, her back to us. Finally, she stops, pivots, then trudges back toward us. She mutters under her breath while scowling at the path between us.

"What has gotten into you today?" Agnus asks.

She doesn't respond and keeps her distance—close enough to be in the picture but apart from the rest of us. We pose awkwardly while Sid takes several pictures, then he returns my phone.

I check the pictures. Bea isn't smiling. Not sure what to make of her change in attitude, I walk to the side of the path, pretending to admire some wildflowers.

Sid does the same. We stare at the landscape before us, trying not to listen to Agnus's and Bea's conversation.

"Will you take a picture of me to send to my folks?" Sid asks.

Thankful for a distraction, I take his phone.

He points to the Kissing Camels with one hand, propping his other hand on his hip. He curves his mouth into his trademark crooked smile. His face flushes, either from embarrassment or the heat. Either way, his parents will love the picture. With his dark hair and height, I wonder ... if Dave and I had had a son, would he have looked like Sid? We wanted more kids, but a necessary hysterectomy squashed that dream.

I give Sid his phone, and we continue our trek to the next formation.

The trail takes us a couple hours to complete. We stop a few times to rest and marvel at the view.

Huffing, I ask, "Do you ladies exercise? You all can run circles around me."

"Salsa classes." Delores's voice is low and sexy. She snaps her fingers above her head. "Every Tuesday."

"Don't forget our water aerobics class on Fridays." Bea finally joins the conversation.

"When we get back, we'll sign you up, Sarah," Agnus says. "You'll love it."

"I'm sure I will. Thank you." Joining a gym or exercise class has been a lonely endeavor in the past. Making friends at the gym never worked out. Either the women already had their workout friends and weren't interested in making more, or they wanted to do their workouts without chitchat. My steps are lighter as we continue along the trail.

Sid's phone dings. He takes it from his back pocket and checks the message. "My mom loves the picture, ma'am." He glances at me. "Thanks for taking it."

"Of course." I smile at him. "Do you talk to your mom often?"

"About every other day," he says. "She worries if I don't call."

The green goblin of jealousy hops on my shoulder, pinging questions I ask myself daily. Why doesn't Emma call me? Wasn't I a good mother? Doesn't she miss me? Did I raise her to be independent, or indifferent?

Someone gives my shoulder a tender squeeze, and I pivot to see who touched me. With a slight smile on her lips, Delores keeps her hand on me. Her light-blue eyes express compassion and warmth. After a few more seconds, she lowers her arm to her side, shifting her gaze to the view below us. The simple gesture chases away the green goblin, but I wonder—do my facial expressions give away my thoughts?

Down the path, Bea and Agnus argue over another rock formation.

"I'm telling you, I don't see it," Bea says.

Agnus takes Bea's head between her hands, then tilts it. "See the tall, thin peaks? Those are the Cathedral Spires." Agnus huffs. Bea shakes her head emphatically.

Agnus releases her head, shrugs, and declares, "I give up."

"There's one more formation we should see," Sid says. "It's not far from here, but it will take a while for us to walk there. I recommend we drive."

The cool northern breeze is gone, leaving the heat of the sun to bear down on us. Wiping sweat from our foreheads, we agree to his suggestion.

True to his word, the ride is short—not enough time for the truck's air conditioning to cool the cab. Once we're back on a trail, Agnus pulls out the park map. She reads while we stare at the huge boulder precariously positioned above a rock pedestal. "This is Balanced Rock. It weighs approximately one-point-four million pounds and rises thirty-five feet above the smaller rock below it."

When she finishes, we climb and squat on the ledge beneath the boulder. While the gigantic red rock formation is amazing, the panoramic overlook steals my breath. Scrubby green bushes, Black-Eyed Susans, and other various wildflowers fill the landscape. Scattered cacti in all shapes and sizes grow around us. In the distance, snowcapped mountains stand proud. All five of us settle onto the red clay ledge. No one lifts a phone to snap a picture. No one speaks.

My muscles relax. How long has it been since I've focused only on the present—not obsessing about the past or worrying about the future? I can't remember.

Delores is the first to rise. She moves under a portion of the Balancing Rock and places her hands under the large boulder. "Look, I'm holding it up. Take my picture." She laughs.

I rise. From this angle, it does look like she's holding the massive rock up with her tiny arms. Delores gives me a cheesy smile, and I snap her picture.

Bea, Sid, and Agnus join us. "I want a picture." Bea sounds happier than she has all day.

I take several pictures of Bea, then Agnus. Sid wants one too. His large frame is dwarfed by the boulder.

Delores takes my phone. "Now it's your turn."

I flex my imaginary biceps while pretending to lift the boulder. My smile comes naturally. Today has been good.

A friendly tourist offers to take a group picture of us in front of the rock. We shuffle into place, with Sid in the center. This time, Bea stands with us.

We dust off our shorts and head back to Sid's truck. Along the way, Bea says, "I'm starving."

"Me too," Agnus agrees.

My stomach growls at the mention of food.

Delores chuckles.

Once we're buckled in our seats, Sid shifts the truck into gear. "Where would you like me to drop you off?"

"Where do you like to eat, Sid?" Bea asks. "Pick well, because you're coming with us. And we're paying."

"We won't take no for an answer." Agnus pauses. "Unless you have other plans."

Sid's face lights up and a blush covers his cheeks.

"I'd be honored," he says softly. "I can't wait to tell my folks about the gracious ladies I spent the day with."

He drives us to a small mom-and-pop-style diner. The outside is a little underwhelming, but inside, it's spotless and inviting. "They serve home cooking like my mom makes." Sid smiles.

The waitress leads us to a table and hands each of us a menu. After she walks away, Bea places hers on the table. She mutters something unintelligible under her breath. "Sid, I need to apologize to you," she says with a strained voice.

He jerks his head up from his menu to stare at Bea.

Her chin quivers. "I'm sorry I've been so hard on you today. I know this doesn't make any sense, but you remind me of my son, Teddy. Your mannerisms, your looks, and ..." A lone tear streaks down her face. "The way you love your family."

Agnus reaches for her shoulder but stops and hands Bea a napkin instead.

Bea dabs at her eyes. "Thank you for not hugging me." She shoots Agnus a grateful look. "I'd be a blubbering mess if you did."

Agnus nods, tears in her eyes too.

"We had a falling-out a few years ago." Another tear makes a trek down Bea's face. "Most days, I try to rise above my sadness at the situation, but hanging out with you made me think about him—and how much I miss him." She lowers her head. "I'm sorry if I seemed angry. I hope I didn't ruin anyone's day."

Agnus pats Bea's hand. "Of course not, Bea," she says in a soft, reassuring voice.

"We love you, Bea," Delores adds in a tender tone.

"It was a good day." I smile at her.

"I never thought a thing about it, ma'am," Sid replies. "I was just happy to be included in your adventure. Like I said, today was like hanging out with my grandma—times four."

Annoyed Sid thinks I'm old enough to be his grandma, I point a finger at him. "All right, I can't hold it in anymore. I'm not old enough to be your grandma. No disrespect. If you say I remind you of your mom, I can live with that."

Bea snorts.

Delores belts out her booming laugh, and Agnus giggles.

"Well ..." Sid hesitates. "You don't remind me of my mom." His face turns red as he shrugs.

I clutch my chest. My eyes grow wide, and my mouth forms a big *O*.

"W-w-well, not th-that it wouldn't be n-nice to have you for a mom, but she's more of a country woman, and you seem more a city lady." He tries to backpedal from his grandma comment. "I can't imagine you herding cattle or bailing hay. Not that there's anything wrong with not knowing how to do those things." Sweat beads pop out on his forehead.

Beside me, Delores fails to hide her muffled giggles.

"I'm just messing with you, Sid." I grin.

His jaw drops and then the whole table bursts into laughter, except for Sid. He pulls his hat off and wipes the nervous sweat from his face and neck with a napkin, which only makes us laugh harder. He smiles weakly, then chuckles.

We finish our meal with pie, then Sid drives us back to the motel. Agnus hands him the wad of cash we pooled together at the diner when he wasn't looking.

"I can't take that much," he protests.

"You earned it." Agnus presses it into his hand.

"We want you to have it," Bea says.

"You can buy yourself a running board." Delores winks at him. "Your grandma will appreciate it."

He laughs, then sets up the stepladder and helps us dismount from the cab one more time. I'm the last one to exit. I climb down the stepladder, fold it up, and hand it to him. "Something to remember us by."

Back in our motel room, I'm the last to get a shower. I take my time, enjoying the steamy water. When I come out of the bathroom, the "girls" are asleep. I lie down with my phone, contentedly scrolling through today's photos. My finger stops on the picture of Bea squatting beneath Balancing Rock. She was trying to be funny, gritting her teeth while pretending to hold up the boulder. We all laughed when I took the picture, but looking at it now, my heart hurts, knowing the real weight she carries.

# CHAPTER EIGHTEEN

Once again, we gather in the motel lobby with the other passengers, hopeful today will be the day we get back on the road to Las Vegas. Suitcases in all shapes and sizes overtake the small entryway.

Bob blocks the door to the parking lot. "Ladies!"

Laughter and talking drown out his shout.

He inhales a deep breath. "Ladies, I need your attention! We have a problem." He's louder this time.

Everyone in the small area stops talking, some mid-sentence. We all focus on him, waiting for his news.

"The bus is going to take longer to fix than we thought."

A rumble of groaning and mumbling fills the air.

Bob hangs his hands on his hips until the group quiets again. "Unfortunately, we will not be able to complete our trip to Las Vegas."

The women erupt into chatter, talking over each other. "What will happen now? Will we receive a refund? How will we get home?"

"This isn't what I signed up for," someone bellows.

Bob raises his hand to get our attention again, but he's lost control.

A loud whistle blares behind me, making my eardrums ring. I spin around to see who it came from.

It's Bea. With two fingers in her mouth, she takes in another deep breath, preparing to blast us all again.

I cover my ears this time, but Agnus shakes her head at Bea. The talking has stopped.

Bob rubs his neck, his blond hair damp from the sweat on his forehead. With a heavy sigh, he says, "I know you all are disappointed. I'm frustrated too. I've been up all night trying to figure out how to continue our trip. It's just not possible. Reservations for the rest of the trip could not be rescheduled, so we had to cancel them. You will get a partial refund. We have one of our other buses coming to take you home. The bus left Missouri last night, so it should be here soon. Until then, make yourselves comfortable."

Resigned, the ladies scuffle along without direction, unsure where to go until the bus arrives. Some people return to their rooms and some sit in the breakfast area, while others find benches outside.

Hands stuffed in his pockets, Bob walks over to us. His gaze moves from Delores to Agnus to Bea, then rests on me. "I am truly sorry," he says with a heavy sigh. "I hope this doesn't deter you from traveling with us again."

"Things happen. We understand." Agnus taps his shoulder. "I'm sure you did all you could."

I nod, but my stomach is tied in knots. I'm not ready to go home.

"Thank you for understanding." He walks on to talk to the other passengers hanging out in the lobby.

"We might as well go back to the diner while we wait," Agnus says.

None of us respond, but we file in line behind her, dragging our luggage across the parking lot with frowns.

We're a different crew entering the diner this morning. A bunch of sad sacks have replaced the giggling, joke-cracking, storytelling women of yesterday.

Delores props an elbow on the table, holding her head in one hand as she stirs her coffee with the other.

Agnus stares vacantly out the nearby window.

Bea sits expressionless eating the slice of pie she ordered.

I try to eat mine, but each dry bite threatens to gag me. My stomach churns, protesting the food. I throw a napkin over my pie and shove it away.

The diner door swings open, and Bob steps in. "The bus is here. Time to leave."

My eyes dart from one lady to the next as they roll their luggage toward the door. My pulse quickens. I follow them. The old, familiar throbbing begins to pound in my temples.

The new bus looms in front of the motel as passengers hand their luggage to Frank, then line up to climb into the bus.

Shuffling from the diner, we are last. Delores, Agnus, and Bea hand their suitcases to Frank and get in line to board the bus. He chucks their luggage into the cargo area, then turns to me.

I pant shallow breaths as panic grips my heart. Without looking at me, Frank grabs the handle on my bag. My fingers wrap around them tighter. When he pulls one direction, I pull the opposite. He stops pulling, but he keeps his hand on the handle. He pivots, locks eyes with me, and frowns. My heart races.

My second hand joins the first. A muscle in his jaw clenches, then he pulls with more force.

Knees bent and using all my weight, I hold on with every

ounce of strength I possess. I glance at the bus, hoping for assistance.

An audience of wide-eyed women peer out the window. Agnus, Bea, and Delores stand on the pavement with worry lines across their foreheads, watching Frank and me in a tug-of-war match. Agnus's mouth gapes open.

"Ma'am, you have to let go," Frank hollers.

"I can't," I cry, my voice choked with emotion.

Bob runs toward us. "What's the problem here?"

The bus driver releases his grip on my suitcase, sending me sprawling onto my back. I wrap my arms around the suitcase now perched on my chest.

"She won't give me her suitcase," Frank says, exacerbated.

Bob extends his hand to help me and pulls me back onto my feet. He reaches for my suitcase, but I take a step back, placing it on the ground behind me.

"I'm not going home," I mutter.

Bob motions for me to come closer.

I stand my ground. "I'm not going home," I repeat louder. "Not yet. I can't."

Bob treads toward me with caution, reminding me of a clip I once saw of Steve Irwin approaching a crocodile. Bob puts his hand on my shoulder. My muscles tense, so he quickly removes his hand. "What's going on, Sarah?" His voice is full of compassion. His kind eyes cause a flood of emotions.

A dam breaks inside me. Hot, painful tears stream down my cheeks. Bob grabs a handkerchief from his pocket and hands it to me.

I dab my eyes, but the tears won't stop. Choked up, I ask with a raspy voice, "Have you ever acted like you're fine, but you're not?"

He pinches his mouth into a tight grimace.

"Something deep down in me broke the night I bought the

ticket for this trip. I don't know what broke or how to fix it—or if it's even fixable. The thing I do know is that I can't go back like this. If I go home now, it might be the end of my marriage and my relationship with my daughter."

Exhausted, my body slumps.

Bob continues to stare at me, the color drained from his face. I'm not sure if he's waiting to see if I'm finished with my confession, or if he has no idea what to say after my tirade. Probably the latter.

We both whirl at the sound of a car creeping by. The driver gawks at us. Blinded by my tears, I forgot we were standing in the middle of a parking lot with an audience.

Bob clears his throat. "Sarah, I can't leave you here." He seems to dismiss my soul-bearing ramblings. "How will you get home? Where will you go? I'm responsible for you."

A lump rises in my throat, strangling me. I second-guess my decision. I'm not this person. I always follow the rules and don't create scenes. I do what others expect of me. I'm the most agreeable person I know.

I bow my head, and my shoulders slump. It takes me a moment to force my hand to grab my suitcase, and then I take a step toward the bus.

Bob lets out a deep breath. He smiles, coaxing my surrender.

Frank motions for my suitcase.

I wither, ready to comply—until the memory of the empty calendar on the kitchen table slaps me out of my people-pleasing trance. An adrenaline rush gushes upward through my chest, burning my ears. Raising my fists to the sky, I yell, "Is no one listening to me? I said I'm not getting on that bus!"

"I don't want to go home either," someone behind me hollers.

I turn to see Delores.

"Ladies, come on." Bob throws up his arms. "Let's just get on the bus and head home." When we don't budge, he groans. "You don't want my boss to reprimand me, do you? I'm responsible for you."

"I am responsible for me. I've been taking care of myself for years now," Delores says bitingly. "Sarah and I will have each other."

Bob steps closer. Worry lines gather around his eyes and forehead.

"I know you mean well, Bob." Delores softens. "We can write a statement for you to take back to your office if that will help."

He pauses. The defeated expression on his face confirms he knows he's beat. He pulls out his wallet from his back pocket and hands me his business card. With a raised eyebrow, he leans closer, pointing to a phone number. "This is my cell number if you need anything." He shoves his wallet back into his pocket. "I would *appreciate* a call when you make it home."

"Of course," I say, grateful.

Delores walks back to Frank and the open compartment.

"Please hand me my luggage, sir," she commands.

Frank looks at Bob, who shrugs and nods.

After rummaging through the stacked luggage, Frank hands Delores her suitcase. With a pleased smile, she rolls her luggage on the pavement and stands beside me.

Agnus and Bea run over to us.

"Aw, come on. Not you too." Bob shakes his head.

"No. We are going home, Bob. Just wanted to say goodbye for now to our friends," Bea says.

"You're welcome to join us," I say.

Agnus gives me a pensive smile. "I need to head home. My grandkids miss me. They keep texting me saying as much. I'm missing them too."

Delores and I both offer a nod of understanding, then turn our attention to Bea.

"I better go with Agnus and keep her company on the trip home. Who knows—the bus may break down again, and I wouldn't want her to be alone." Bea takes Agnus's hand and gives it a light squeeze.

We hug each other. In only a few days, these women have become cherished friends. "Thank you for including me on your adventure." My voice cracks. "You don't know how much it has meant to me. I'm going to miss you both."

"This isn't the last time you'll see us," Bea assures me. "You're one of us now." She tugs the wide-brimmed hat on my head and turns, but not before I see unshed tears glisten in her eyes.

"As soon as you two get back, we'll plan lunch together." Agnus's bright smile and rosy cheeks light up her face. "We'll want to hear all about the rest of your trip." She gives me another hug, this one longer than before, then she spins around and follows Bea onto the bus.

Frank shuts the luggage compartment door, then he and Bob disappear into the bus. The door closes behind them.

Delores and I remain standing next to our luggage, waving until the bus is out of view.

"What's the plan, Sarah?" Delores looks at me expectantly.

"Plan?"

# CHAPTER NINETEEN

"Can we take a moment to regroup?" The question comes out shriller than I intended.

Delores nods, points to the diner, and starts pulling her luggage behind her. I follow. Once again, we are at the booth where we ate breakfast. The waitress gives us a confused look but brings us menus and water anyway.

"Take your time planning our next move," Delores says. "I'm going to check out the gift shop." She winks, then disappears into an attached room. She seems unbothered by this recent turn of events, while I can't quit biting my lower lip.

I know I should call Dave and tell him what I've done, but the dread filling the pit of my stomach holds me back.

The waitress returns and asks what I want.

"Just water, thank you." I smile at her.

She scowls, then grabs the menus, most likely annoyed we've taken a table from a paying customer. Throwing my purse over my shoulder, I vacate the booth before my water arrives. With a handle in each hand, I pull Delores's and my luggage toward the gift shop.

The wheels rumble across the tiled floor, drawing the remaining customers' attention until I enter the small gift store.

Delores swings around from the counter. Her face glows with excitement. "Look what I found for our bracelets," she shouts louder than necessary in the tight quarters. "Cancan-girl charms. Aren't they the perfect addition?" Without waiting for my reaction, she swivels back to the cashier. "I'll take two."

She chatters back and forth with the cashier, telling her bits and pieces about our time dancing on the stage.

I stand immobilized, staring at an array of wooden signs with various platitudes hanging on the wall behind the cash register. Some signs display funny sayings, while others feature inspirational quotes. My eyes dart from one sign to another, hoping for the one that reads, "You need to do this." But none of them do.

Delores moves over to me, holding one of the charms in her palm.

My gaze veers from the signs to the charm—a silver lady with a glittery purple dress. One of her legs is extended into a high kick. When I don't take the charm, Delores pulls up my arm and latches it onto my bracelet. Once she's checked it's secure, she drops my arm. She adds the other charm to her bracelet.

She twists her wrist from side to side. "Look, she's dancing."

I stare at her wrist, unable to process her words amidst the myriad of thoughts attacking my brain.

Delores stops rotating her wrist and lifts my chin until my eyes meet hers. She raises an eyebrow. "You know, we could go check out the Grand Canyon."

Nausea hits the pit of my stomach. I clasp my middle, afraid I might retch all over Delores. Realization knocks the air from my lungs. I've not only stranded myself, but her too. Once I've pushed down the bile rising in my throat, I say with a tremor, "I've made a terrible mistake. We should have ridden the bus home." I squeeze my eyes shut, but my mind spirals like the dust devils we saw in Kansas. Finally settling on one thought, I say, "Let me call Dave. He'll know what to do."

With an unbelievably strong grip, Delores grabs my shoulders, rescuing me from a full-on panic attack. I open my eyes to her penetrating stare only inches away. She takes a deep breath. "You didn't make a mistake. You're just afraid." Her firm tone leaves no room for argument.

The imaginary elephant on my chest makes breathing difficult. "I've never been on my own before." My voice trembles. "I have no idea what to do."

She remains unmovable, gripping my shoulders harder. Her pale-blue eyes flash, reminding me of a summer thunderstorm speeding over the ocean. "First of all, you are not on your own. You have me. And second, it's about time you did some things on your own. What if something happens to Dave? Are you going to curl up into a ball and die?" Her words slap me from my mental fog. What *would* I do?

When I don't reply, she releases a long, heavy sigh, letting me know she's disappointed. She removes her hands from my shoulders. The storm in her eyes is gone before she breaks eye contact and mutters, "Let's find out when the next Greyhound bus leaves for home." She whirls to face the cashier. "Do you have a bus schedule?"

Delores's bitter smile of resignation lights a fire in my chest. She's right. I'm scared—I've been scared my whole life. Right here and now, I decide I don't want to be scared any longer.

Marching to the counter, I yank the bus schedule from Delores's fingers. "We won't be needing this." I hand it back to the cashier and smile at Delores. "But we do need to rent a car and buy an atlas."

Delores claps her hands, then lifts a palm for a high five. Our hands smack together as her red lips stretch into a grin so bright, it could light up a pitch-black night—no moon or stars.

The cashier gives us directions to the only rental-car business in town. There are no taxis to call. Lucky for us, the place is only half a mile away.

We leave the gift shop and begin our trek. The sun scorches us as we walk along the shoulder of the interstate, dragging our luggage behind us. I'm wearing lightweight bermuda shorts, a T-shirt, and tennis shoes, but Delores is in her usual dress pants, silk blouse, and wedges.

She giggles and waves when a passing trucker honks at us. I don't appreciate the unwanted attention, so I pick up the pace. By the time we reach the car rental, we're both drenched in sweat. My flat-ironed hair that I worked into submission this morning is now frizzy and bushy, reminding me of the wool on an alpaca's head. Though Delores's silk blouse hugs her body, somehow her hair still looks like she stepped out of a high-end salon.

Thankfully, the cashier called ahead for us. "The owner's name is Tony," she informed us. "He said you girls were real lucky. He only has one more car available."

Bells clang when we enter the one-room trailer parked in the middle of nowhere. Wood-paneled walls and lime-green shag carpet transport me back to my grandma's house in the seventies. Behind a brown metal desk sits a big man in a white short-sleeved dress shirt. A portable fan blows on his face, but his slicked-back gray hair never moves. The name plate on his desk reads "Tony Clarke."

"You ladies must be from the diner." He extends an

enormous hand to us, and we each shake it. "Did Joan relay my message? We only have one car on the lot for rent."

We both nod.

"I have to admit, she's a beaut—and reliable," he adds.

"Sounds great." Delores hands him her driver's license and insurance card. "Anything else you need?" During our walk here, she insisted she would take care of the car.

After filling out the rental agreement, Tony stands. "Now for the big reveal." He takes us through the back door of the trailer. Our luggage wheels scrape against the white chat of the parking lot as we hurry to keep up with him.

"Oh my." Delores abandons her suitcase in the middle of the lot and sprints to a classic cherry-red Mustang convertible. There's a pony on the chrome grill and raised white letters on the tires.

"What year is it?" she asks, still staring at the car.

"A 1973." Tony's chest seems to expand, along with his height.

"I thought so." Her lips lift into a dreamy smile.

"You like it?" he asks.

"If you tell me this is what we're renting, I may have to kiss you right on the lips," she says, still admiring the car.

Tony's face burns red, but his smile widens. "I'm afraid it's not. Your car is over there." He points to a silver compact SUV. We both look over at our rental, then Delores's gaze returns to the Mustang.

"Get in," Tony says.

"Really?" Her eyes dance.

Tony waves his hand toward the car and nods.

Delores strides over to the driver's side. She opens the door, runs a careful hand over the white leather upholstery, then slides into the bucket seat. Immense pleasure spreads across her face as her hands grip the steering wheel. "Come on, Sarah."

I check for Tony's approval. When he nods, I run around to the other side of the car, eager to jump into the passenger seat. The chrome on the dash shines. I keep my hands in my lap, afraid I'll mar the interior of the car.

Delores peers at Tony and points to the keys in the ignition. He glances at our luggage and purses lying behind him, then says, "Okay, but leave it in park."

Delores squeals, rubs her hands together, then twists the key. The engine roars to life and transitions to a loud, slow rumble, vibrating from the power of the engine. She leans back in her seat, her hands remaining on the steering wheel as she shuts her eyes. Her lips spread into a nostalgic smile.

Tony motions for me to turn on the radio. With a flick of the silver knob, Aretha Franklin croons from the speakers. Delores sways gently, her voice joining in, soft and low.

Tony and I remain still, watching her enjoy this moment. She's oblivious to our presence, transported to another time and place. But as the song continues, her facial expression changes. Her smile falters and a lone tear falls down her cheek. With her eyes still shut, she sings along with "Until You Come Back to Me (That's What I'm Gonna Do)." Before the second verse begins, Delores opens her eyes and twists the silver knob. Silence fills the air as she uses the back of her hand to swipe at the wetness on her cheeks. "Well, this has been fun, but we must be on our way," she says in a stilted tone. "Wouldn't you agree, Sarah?"

Tony and I exchange confused glances.

"Thank you, Tony. It's a beautiful car." Delores bolts out of the convertible. Once she reaches her luggage, she lugs it toward our rental.

Tony and I follow her. She opens the back hatch and

throws in her suitcase with unexpected force. The rear of the SUV bounces. Seeming not to notice, she strides to the passenger side, seats herself, then slams the door.

Tony's brows draw together. Worry lines ripple on his forehead.

"I promise we'll take good care of the car," I say, trying to reassure him.

I shake his hand, load my belongings next to her suitcase, and close the back hatch with care.

Tony hasn't moved from where I left him. He rests his hands on his hips, the worry lines across his face still present.

I wave and smile, then climb into the driver's seat.

Delores stares straight ahead.

We need to get out of here before Tony changes his mind and takes back his rental.

I don't ask Delores about her dramatic mood swing, deciding it's best to leave it alone. I wish I had her knack for reading minds. I start the engine and crank the air conditioner to full blast.

Eyes locked on the windshield, Delores doesn't move, though the gust from the vent lifts and stirs her bangs.

"We still on for the Grand Canyon?" I ask timidly.

Finally, she turns to me and says, "Absolutely."

# CHAPTER TWENTY

Delores points to the highway sign ahead for the southern rim. We continue to drive a short distance, then I shift the steering wheel to the left and pull into the parking lot. Night still lingers outside the back window, but through Delores's passenger window, a yellow-and-orange globe slowly rises on the horizon.

She unlatches her seat belt, then looks at me. "Where's your picture?"

I lower the sun visor, and the old Polaroid falls into my lap. Carefully, I pick it up to hand it to Delores. She grabs her white wide-brimmed hat from the floorboard and places it on her head. After lowering her visor, she checks her reflection in the attached mirror. She angles her head right, then left before exiting the car, clutching my photo.

I grab the Arizona ball cap I purchased at the last gas station and pull my hair through the hole in the back. I run to catch up. A thin layer of sweat covers the nape of my neck.

Together, we walk out to a cliff edge. I suck in my breath when my eyes take in the enormity of the canyon. Delores picks up a large rock and throws it with all her might. We listen intently as it bounces from one jagged ledge to another. The knocking of the rock seems endless until we hear a final distant thud below. The blue-green Colorado River snakes along the canyon floor. A high-pitched screech pierces the air. We look up as a bald eagle soars above, riding an updraft across the canyon.

I glance at Delores. She's removed her sun hat. With her eyes closed, she lifts her face toward the sun's rays. I mirror her. With the warmth of the sun on my face and a slight breeze at my back, time seems to stop.

"Doesn't this make you feel so ..." At the sound of Delores's voice, I open my eyes.

She waves her arm from the left to the right of the panoramic view before us.

I fill in the word I think she's looking for. "Small?"

"Yes, that too. But I was going to say grateful." She smiles as she gazes out at the vastness around us. "Grateful to be here —in this place, at this time—with you." Her eyes sparkle as she turns to me.

I ponder her words in my heart, touched by her comment. We stand together in silence, awed by the view. The colors change as the sun rises, casting its light across the canyon and rock formations. Various shades of orange, brown, russet, purple, and yellow are on full display.

Delores takes my photo from her pocket and walks along the rim. She stops several times to hold the photo up, comparing it to the scenery behind it.

"I'm not sure I can find the exact spot this picture was taken, but this looks close." She motions me over to her. "See how the river winds below, only partially in view behind that huge rock?"

I glance from the photo to the canyon. "Maybe? I don't know. Landscapes can change."

Delores's face falls. "Maybe?"

Seeing her disappointment, I offer, "It could be."

"It is. I know it is." She smiles with confidence. "Let me take your picture in that same spot."

I'm not convinced, but I allow her to move me into the space she claims is where I stood in the photo. She pulls her phone out of her back pocket and snaps my picture. "Let's take one more." She joins me. Lifting her phone above our heads at an angle, she snaps a selfie with the Grand Canyon in the background. "Do you remember being here with your mom and dad?" she asks.

"No," I say sadly. "I guess I was too little. My memory doesn't go that far back."

"I'm sorry. I was hoping coming here would help trigger it," Delores admits.

"Me too. It would have been nice to remember when we were a family. My parents divorced when I was five or six." I'm grateful she doesn't push for more information, but a hole the size of this canyon fills my heart. Missing something I never had or someone I never knew is a peculiar feeling.

Still holding my photo, she flips it over. "Whose address is this on the back?"

I lean in. The writing has faded, but it's readable. "I don't know." I shrug. "This picture was in a box of my dad's stuff. He passed away several years ago. I tucked his things in my basement. I kept meaning to go through them but never got around to it until recently." The memory of wedding paraphernalia scattered all over the living room floor seems like a lifetime ago.

"It's an Arizona address. We should check it out." Delores the sleuth returns.

"I'm not sure that's a good idea." I'm uneasy. "Who knows whose address it is or why it's on the back of this photo."

"It could be a long-lost relative," Delores says, trying to entice me.

"Or it could be a serial killer."

She snorts at my sarcastic reply.

I shake my head at her, then slip the picture into my back pocket. High in the sky, the sun beats down on us. With the temperature rising and the breeze gone, we decide to check out the air-conditioned visitor center. We both buy a book filled with photos of panoramic views of the Grand Canyon, plus some snacks and drinks for the road.

The sweltering heat discourages us from walking any more trails. Instead, we return to our rental car. The steering wheel burns my hands when I grip it, so we sit, not touching anything until the air conditioner cools the inside of the SUV.

Delores is silent but keeps sneaking glances at me from the corner of her eye. It's obvious what she wants, and she knows how to use her charm to persuade me. I'm a little curious to find out who lives at the address written on the back of the photo but also afraid of what I might discover.

"I asked the guy at the counter how far the town written on the back of your photo is. He said it's only a couple hours away," Delores hints.

"I'm sure it's a dead end," I say.

"It might be." She pauses. "But what if it's not?" Her tone rises.

Agitated, I ask, "Did you always get your way with your husband?"

"Of course." She winks and flashes me a smug smile.

I exhale a tense sigh. "Okay."

With one eyebrow raised, she asks, "Okay?"

"Yes, whatever." I roll my eyes.

Delores claps her hands. Her bangles chime as they clang against each other.

"I'll drive," she says.

Before I can object, she jumps out of the car and runs around to my side. Why not? Her name is on the rental, after all.

We trade seats, and Delores taps her palm against the steering wheel. Once she's confirmed it's cooled, she bends her ringed fingers around it and shifts the SUV into reverse, then drive. "Can you find us some cruising music?" She points to the radio.

I tap the search button. The tuner stops several times, but only blaring static comes through the speakers. After a few minutes of manually turning the dial left, then right, I find a clear station and give a thumbs-up. She grins at me. I'm pleased with such a silly accomplishment, but it's short-lived. My insides churn more with each slow, sad song.

Delores doesn't seem to mind. She hums along with the radio while I watch the solitary desert through my window.

After ten minutes, I turn to her and ask, "Why didn't you go home with Agnus and Bea?"

She stops humming but continues to focus straight ahead as she drives.

My boldness makes me blush, but I don't back down. Another sad, sappy song comes on.

Delores lowers the volume and glances at me. "I wasn't ready to go back to my empty house."

"Oh," I manage to say around the thick lump in my throat. My thoughts shift to Dave.

Delores turns the table on me. "Why didn't you go back, Sarah?" She gives me one of her piercing stares.

I gulp. My mind races as I search for the words to explain

what's going on in my heart and head. But there aren't any. "I need answers, but I'm not sure what the questions are."

She gives me a thoughtful look. "Maybe that's what this trip is about—finding answers to your unspoken questions."

"Maybe," I whisper, sinking lower into my seat.

Delores hums again, her eyes set on the horizon before us. Her soft tone, the whirring of the tires rolling on the highway, and the cool air from the vent blowing on my face relaxes me. My eyes drift shut, and I dream of a faceless woman with auburn hair.

# CHAPTER TWENTY-ONE

### A Childhood Memory

A yellow-orange stream of light lowers through the kitchen window as the sun sets. I sit at our kitchen table, tracing invisible circles on the weathered oak with my finger as I wait. Dad walks into the kitchen, probably checking on me.

"Your favorite show's on. Want to come watch it with me?" His smile and wink are meant to entice me.

"No, I'm okay. I don't want to get mussed up. Mom should be here soon," I say.

Worry lines crease the edges of his hazel eyes. He nods, then fills a glass with water from the sink.

I haven't seen my mom in several weeks. At first, she came to get me every weekend, then it became every other weekend, now maybe once a month.

Dad walks back to the table and sits next to me. With a deck of cards in his hands, he asks, "How about a hand of Rummy?"

"No. I'm okay, Dad. Really." I place my small hand on top of his larger one. He envelops my hand in his big warm palm. My racing heart slows. Being on my best behavior for my mother always makes me nervous. I'm not a bad kid, but I never want to give her a reason not to spend time with me.

We sit together in silence, straining our ears for her car in the driveway. After several minutes, Dad says, "You look so pretty, Sarah. I like the new dress your grandma bought you." He smiles at me.

I return a partial smile, then look down at my navy-blue dress with white trim piping around the collar and sleeves. Grandma spent a lot of money on my dress, and I'm grateful.

A blurry reflection of myself stares back at me from the polished surface of my Mary Jane shoes. I pat my strawberry-blonde hair to ensure it has not escaped the tightly woven braids secured with matching navy ribbons. My mother should be pleased with my hair when she picks me up. In the past, she's commented how unruly it is and complained that she can't do anything with it. She is beautiful, with sleek dark-auburn hair and almond-shaped brown eyes. I love my dad but secretly hope I look just like her when I grow up.

My pink overnight bag sits at my feet. I pick it up and check that I haven't forgotten something for the umpteenth time.

Dad says nothing as I pull my clothes out, refold them, then return them to my bag. Finished, I place the bag back on the floor. My eyes rise to my dad's scowling face. A muscle twitches on his jawline. He pours a glass of lemonade from the pitcher on the counter, hands it to me, and walks to the living room. Dialogue and suspenseful music blare from the TV. The recliner groans under his weight.

The excitement of seeing my mother dwindles as the sun sets through the kitchen window. I'm left with a weight too big for a small girl.

My eyelids grow heavy. Crossing my arms on the table for a pillow, I lay my head down. Dad's laughter carries from the living room. It comforts me, lulling me to sleep.

I have a hazy memory of my dad's strong arms lifting me from the chair and laying me gently in my bed. Soft blankets are tucked around me. Somewhere between consciousness and unconsciousness, I remember I'm wearing my new dress and hate that it will be wrinkled before my mother sees me in it.

The next morning, the fragrant smells of sweet maple syrup and salty bacon wake me. Wiping the sleep from my eyes, I walk to our kitchen. Grandma sits at the table.

"I am not putting her through that anymore." Dad slams several pancakes onto a plate. "Never again."

Grandma notices me in the doorway and motions me closer. She scoops me up to sit on her lap.

Dad's eyes meet mine, and he clears his throat. His face softens. After walking across the creaky hardwood floor, he plants a kiss on the top of my head. "Good morning, sweet pea." He smiles as a flush creeps across his cheeks.

He retrieves our filled plates from the counter and sets them before us. I move over to the seat beside Grandma. My braids have fallen out, my navy dress is rumpled, and I have no idea what happened to my shoes. Grandma pats my knee, then discusses the weekend weather with Dad. No one mentions last night—or my mother.

# CHAPTER TWENTY-TWO

The present

My growling stomach wakes me. "I'm hungry." I yawn as I stretch my arms. I glance out the window and notice the landscape hasn't changed. Miles and miles of desert stretch as far as I can see.

"Me too." Delores sounds stressed. "But more importantly, we need gas." She points to the fuel gauge.

I lean over and peek at the dashboard. My heart races at the glowing warning light. The red indicator points to *E*.

"I should have filled up at the last station, but I didn't want to stop and wake you. I thought there would be more gas stations along the way," she says.

"I'm sorry, Delores. I shouldn't have fallen asleep. I was just so—"

The engine sputters.

Our rental decelerates, the speedometer dropping from sixty miles per hour to fifty, then forty, thirty, twenty, ten. The steering wheel locks. Delores white-knuckles it, pulling the unwilling SUV to the right. She manages to maneuver us onto the shoulder before the vehicle powers down.

We scan our surroundings. There isn't a house, business, rest stop, electric line, or any sign of civilization anywhere. And no satellite tower in sight.

"Do you have any bars on your cell?" Delores asks.

"Only one." I grimace at my phone. "Pray it's enough to check the map app for the nearest gas station." Pinching the screen out to zoom, I see the tiny map shows nothing for miles. I shake my head at Delores.

"Can you call a tow truck, triple A, something?" Delores suggests.

Staring at the red bar reading 3 percent at the top of my cell screen, I scowl. "I didn't charge my phone last night. Did you?"

She rustles through her purse, frantically searching. After emptying the contents, Delores throws her arm in the air, her rhinestone-covered cell in the palm of her hand. "I found it." Her brief celebration is dashed when she can't get her phone to power on. "I can't believe it. Mine's dead. I must have forgotten to charge my phone too."

What to do? We can't take off walking in the desert. The only answer I can come up with is to call Dave, but what if he doesn't pick up? He could be in a meeting or, worse yet, still mad enough not to answer my call. Will he even be able to hear me if he does answer? Staring at the single bar on the top of my screen, I cup my phone between my hands in a prayerful pose. Here goes nothing. I tap on contacts and scroll down the list of names until Dave's picture appears on the screen. It rings once on my end.

"Hello, Sarah."

The power bar at the top of my phone flashes 2 percent. My chest tightens. Knowing I only have a few minutes before my phone dies, words rush from my mouth. "Dave, I have to talk fast. We need—"

"When are you coming home? We need to talk."

"Please, Dave, just listen!" I shriek, watching the red power line shrink.

"What's go ... on?" His voice changes from anger to his levelheaded "don't panic" tone he's used many times. "Are y ... okay?" Even though the signal is weak and some of his words cut out, his tender voice fills me with comfort. I picture him holding the phone while walking around our living room, and an intense ache builds in my stomach. We've never been away from each other this long. I miss him.

"Stay focused!" Delores shouts, snapping me out of my trance.

I raise my voice as if my volume will help with the signal somehow. "I can't talk long. My cell battery is almost dead. We need your help."

"Who's *we?*" Dave asks loud enough for Delores to hear.

"Hello," she says cheerfully.

I give her a side-eye, mouthing "really?"

The red bar seems to flash brighter, faster. Panicked, I shout, "Dave, listen. We ran out of gas in the desert. Can you do a google search and find a tow truck or someone to bring us some gas?"

Delores points to the highway number and mile-marker sign on the shoulder of the road ahead of us. "Give him our location."

I slowly enunciate where we are stalled on the highway. Sweat drips down the sides of my face, either from the increasing heat in the rental or the adrenaline running through my veins. "Did you get that?" I pray he wrote down the information.

"You know, if you didn't run away, you wouldn't be in this predicament."

I grit my teeth. "Do you really think this is the time for a lecture?" Before he can answer, my phone powers down. A black screen replaces the picture of Dave's face.

"Is he calling someone to come get us?" Delores fans herself with the rental contract agreement.

"Of course." I smile while my insides churn. In truth, I have no idea. Instead of taking down our location, he scolded me. Surely concern will win out over his desire to teach me a lesson. Right?

Without air conditioning, the desert heat fills the car, making the stifling air hard to breathe. We decide to exit the car, hoping for a breeze. Delores picks a few desert flowers growing through the rocks and dirt beside the road.

"These are called lupines." She holds a plant with a brown stalk and small purple blooms. She walks farther into the sandy terrain, adding a few yellow flowers to her bouquet. "These are desert poppies," she explains like she's teaching a botany lesson.

I don't care what they are called, but I nod and smile anyway, grateful for the distraction. I'm learning that in addition to her uncanny talent for reading my mind, Delores has a gift for finding the positive in any situation.

The sun begins its slow descent. Shading my eyes with one hand, I squint, scanning both directions. No sign of rescue— only shadows growing across the terrain from the various cacti scattered over the desert floor. A cooler breeze hits the back of my neck, drying some of my sweat. A tumbleweed rolls down the highway and crosses to the other side.

Delores continues her exploration, wandering farther from the car. The distance between us makes me uneasy, but her contented expression as she wanders from plant to plant helps dismiss my fears. My stomach growls, so I head back to our car to find the snacks we bought hours ago. Grabbing them from the back, I notice a worn red, turquoise, and black Aztec blanket under our suitcases. The previous renter must have left it behind.

I lay the blanket out on a bare spot of sand next to the SUV and spill the bags of junk food into the middle. My mouth waters. "Dinner's served," I yell, ringing a pretend dinner triangle in my hand.

Delores nods and strolls back.

"We have candy, chips, and beef jerky." I badly imitate a French chef's accent.

"It's like we're camping, or even better, Girl Scouts earning our outdoor badge." Delores grins. She takes off her wedges and sits on the blanket, one leg crossed over the other. Even barefoot in the middle of the desert, she's glamorous.

"Were you a Girl Scout?" I ask.

"No, but I always wanted to be one. Too many kids in our family for us to have separate interests. We all did the same thing, or none of us did anything." Her smile thins into a straight line. "Being the sixth of ten kids, I usually didn't get a say about much. And no one in our community could keep all of us straight. I was always mistaken for one of my sisters. I hated it. I wanted to stand out, be unique."

Intrigued by the idea of a young Delores, I ask, "So what did you do?"

"My mom's friend Clara sold Avon. She knew we couldn't afford any of it, but as she went door-to-door to sell and make deliveries, she would always stop by our house and give us samples." Delores's full smile returns with a faraway look in her eyes. "I loved the miniature lipsticks in their cute white tubes. My favorite shade was luscious red." We both laugh.

"Hence, your trademark red lipstick." I smile when Delores nods. "What about your sense of style? I love how you dress."

I can't be sure if it's the heat or my compliment, but Delores's usual ivory skin deepens to a pinkish hue. It must be the heat. In our short time together, I've not seen anything embarrass her.

"We were poor. I never got new clothes, just hand-me-downs from my older sisters. But when I turned fourteen, I took a job after school at our local clothing alteration shop." Her tone rises. "I mostly worked the counter, making tickets for whatever alterations the customers needed. When business was slow, Mrs. Woodward, the owner, taught me some basic sewing. There were always stray buttons, broken zippers, or, on an especially good day, some leftover sparkly sequined beads no one wanted. In my knapsack, I would tuck away any items I thought might be useful to embellish my old hand-me-downs. My family and classmates liked to tease me about my eccentric blinged-out outfits, but they quit mixing me up with my sisters." Her face beams as she points to herself. "No one dressed like me. I was one of a kind."

I smile, too, admiring her spunk and ingenuity.

But her smile fades. "My kids say I dress too flashy, especially for a woman my age. I embarrass them." Pain flickers across her face.

Her dejected expression surprises me. Delores strikes me as a woman who doesn't need others' approval. She's the most confident, put-together, fun-loving person I've ever met. I didn't think anyone or anything could put a chink in her self-confidence. But I was wrong.

"What do they know?" I smirk.

She belts out the loud laugh I've come to enjoy. "Yeah, what do they know?" She gives me a grateful nod, then bites into a piece of beef jerky.

A coyote howls nearby. Small hairs rise on the back of my neck. Then a chorus of coyotes yips and barks in high-pitched frequencies, sounding closer than the first howl.

Delores and I scramble to our feet.

"Camping is over," she announces. We grab the four corners of the blanket, our leftovers colliding into the middle. She ties the corners together, then swings the bundle over her shoulder. We race to the car and toss the blanket of food into the back. Then we dive into our seats and lock the doors.

Delores checks her watch. Only a small sliver of sunlight remains on the horizon. Darkness will envelop us soon. "Dave did say he would call a tow truck, right?" Worry lines furrow once again between her brows.

"I'm sure there's one on the way right now," I assure her with a weak smile. At least I hope so.

# CHAPTER TWENTY-THREE

Slowly, my eyes open to a man's voice and loud tapping on the windshield.

"Hello? Hello." A bear of a man stares at me through the glass.

I sit up, rubbing my eyes to see him better. The sun rises on the horizon behind him. I peek at Delores to check if she's awake.

Glittery gold eyes stare back at me. One of the eyes winks. Where did she find a sleep mask?

The man taps again on the glass, drawing my attention back to him. "Hello." His voice grows louder.

I wave at him through the windshield. He stops his incessant tapping and yells, "Are you Sarah Goodwin? I got a call from a Dave Goodwin to tow her car to a gas station."

I nod. My gaze moves from him to a white tow truck parked in front of us with "TD's Towing" painted in large black letters on the back window.

"I would have brought some gas in a jug, but that wouldn't get you far out here. The station is a ways down the road. I thought it would be best to take you there so you can get a full tank."

Delores releases a loud yawn, letting me know she's awake.

The seventy-something man waits by my window, hands tucked in the pockets of his bib overalls.

"What do you think?" I whisper. "Can we trust him?"

Delores removes her sleep mask and eyes the stranger peering through my window. "He looks harmless."

I nod, then shake my head at how refreshed and perfect she looks. Not a hair out of place. I glance in the rearview mirror at my reflection. I wipe the sleep from my eyes and the drool from the corner of my mouth before opening the door to check his credentials.

Delores exits from her side and joins us.

He hands me a business card with the name "Tom Decker" printed in large black letters. He points to the name on the card in my palm, then thumps his chest. "That's me."

"Glad to meet you, Tom. I'm Sarah, and this is Delores."

"Good to meet you too." He shakes our hands. When he breaks out a wide, friendly grin, my shoulders relax.

Blushing, I say, "I can't believe we ran out of gas."

"You would be surprised how many times that happens out here. A lot of people bring an extra container of gas in their trunk to avoid being stranded." The judgment I was expecting doesn't come. Instead, his kind eyes meet mine. "Let's get you some gas." He stops. "Oh, and are you hungry?" My stomach gurgles loud in response. He chuckles. "Next door to the gas station is a diner where the locals hang out. The food's not great, but it's edible." His face scrunches up like a dried prune when he adds, "Stay away from the salmon." I giggle, thinking he's kidding, but he gives me a stern scowl. "No, I'm serious."

"Warning noted." I give him my most serious face.

"And please don't tell Hazel or Sam I said any of this," he whispers.

I nod, and Delores mimes closing an imaginary zipper across her lips, then pretends to throw away a key.

Tom chuckles. Delores giggles. Their gazes lock.

After an awkward stretch of silence, I say, "We checked the map and couldn't find any gas stations nearby. Where is this one, and why isn't on the map?"

"Well, it's just a stop in the road. No post office or town nearby, so you wouldn't find it on a map."

The sun continues to rise, and the temperature with it. Tom pulls out a white handkerchief with a big *T* insignia on the corner and wipes the back of his neck. Then he walks to his truck.

Delores and I take that as our signal to cross to the other side of the road and get out of his way. Tom's truck starts with a loud rumble, then slowly backs up to our rental. I'm surprised how agile he is for an older man. Before long, our lifeless SUV is hooked up to his truck. Once he's secured the rental, he motions for us to climb into the cab.

Getting into a truck with a stranger in the middle of nowhere feels weird. It will be a tight fit for the three of us. Before I can ask Delores if she wants to get in first, she pushes me in front of her, almost knocking me down. Once I regain my balance, I step up into the cab and slide to the middle of the bench seat.

Delores uses the handle to lift herself into the seat next to the window. I look over to her, my eyes wide, and mouth, "what the heck."

A giggle escapes her lips.

Tom hops in on my other side. When he puts the truck into drive, he accidently hits my knee with the metal gear shift.

"Ouch!" My face heats in embarrassment for not stifling my reaction. Delores giggles again. I give her a squinty glare.

"Sorry, ma'am," Tom says.

"It's okay." I sit awkwardly, bumping shoulders with Tom on my left and Delores on my right. Every time I inch closer to Delores, she pushes me toward Tom. Her eyes sparkle with a glint of humor.

An uncomfortable silence swells for several miles. Delores, who is usually a chatter bug, keeps quiet.

Right when I'm about to start a conversation, Tom speaks up. We learn he has three daughters and a son. The daughters all moved away, spread out across the US, but his son stayed home to help Tom with the business. All his kids are married with children. Tom is a grandpa to four granddaughters and five grandsons. He doesn't see them as much as he would like due to the towing business being the only one in the area, but he plans to retire soon. His son will take over. Tom's company has been around for twenty-five years. His wife helped with the bookkeeping until she passed away last year. Her name was Rose. "She was the love of my life." His voices softens and breaks. He swipes at his eyes with the back of his hand. I avert my eyes and glance at Delores, not wanting to embarrass him.

Delores digs around in her purse. She pulls out a tissue and dabs at her eyes while staring out the passenger window. Even though the air-conditioning vent is blowing cool air, a heaviness fills the cab. In the quiet, my thoughts turn to Dave.

# CHAPTER TWENTY-FOUR

Fall Semester—College—Sophomore Year

The first time I set eyes on Dave, I was walking to my college Fundamentals of Art 101 class.

Leaving the sidewalk, I cut across the quad. Wanting to feel the cool green grass beneath my feet, I bend over and slip off my sandals. Once upright again, I see a blur of a man barreling toward me. Unable to move out of his way in time, we collide. He hits me hard, knocking me flat on my back. The contents of my purse scatter everywhere, along with a stack of textbooks from my backpack.

With the wind knocked out of me, I gulp in a big breath of air and yell, "Ouch! Watch where you're going." I slowly roll to a kneeling position and start to gather my loose items.

Dave bends down beside me. "I'm so sorry. Are you all right?" His deep, masculine voice sends a tingle along my spine. When I don't reply, he says, "Here, let me help you," and picks up my lip balm, pens, and wallet from the ground.

Even though my ribs ache from the blow of his body hitting

mine, I mutter, "No," and grab the items from his hand. I throw everything into my purse.

He hands me a book that landed out of my reach. I flip it over from front to back, checking for damage, before cramming it into my backpack.

"I was running late to class," he says. "I thought someone behind me hollered my name. I turned to look and didn't see you." He reaches out to touch my shoulder. "Are you sure you're not hurt?" He sounds genuinely concerned.

I huff, wishing he would just go to class. But it seems he won't leave until I've reassured him that I'm fine. I lift my head, raising my eyes to his. Warm caramel-brown eyes with swirls of gold flecks lock with mine. My heart flip-flops. Transfixed, I watch him run his fingers through his thick, glossy black hair, pulling the front section away from his face. The worry lines gathered on his forehead compel me to assure him I'm not hurt. My lips part, but no words come out.

With his hand still on my shoulder, he gives me a little squeeze, waking me from my stupor. I jerk away from his reach. The lines on his brow deepen.

Plastering a smile on my face, I say, "I'm fine, really."

He blows out a sigh of relief, *and then he smiles*. My insides melt. Heat rushes up my neck into my face. Perspiration pops out across my forehead. Unprepared for the effect his smile has on me, my eyes shoot to my backpack lying on the ground.

He rises and then extends his hand to me.

Not wanting him to feel my sweaty palms, I growl, "I've got it," sounding harsher than I intended.

He retracts his hand and shoves it in his pocket. Slinging my purse over one shoulder and the backpack over the other, I push myself to my feet.

He's at least a foot taller than me. "I'm Dave." He gives me another perfect smile, which rattles me even more.

I'm flustered by the way my insides feel off balance in his presence. Instead of offering him my name, I say, "I'm late," and walk away. I scamper as fast as my bare feet will take me until I'm in the safety of my classroom.

As the professor gives the lecture, my mind drifts off, thinking about my interaction with Dave. I'm ashamed of how rude I was. What got into me?

For weeks after our altercation, I tried not to notice him. On a small campus, it's common to see the same people walking to and from classes, but I'd never seen him before the fated day he ran me over. Now, he was everywhere. Each time I caught his gaze on me, my face would burn. I'd dart my eyes down, pretending not to notice him.

I admit—I liked the attention. Every morning, I took extra time to fix my hair and makeup. I painted my fingernails and toenails. Instead of my usual T-shirts and blue jeans, I wore dresses reserved for special occasions matched with cute boots or sandals. I looked forward to seeing Dave on my way to class, imagining his focus lingering on me as I passed by. But one day, everything changed.

With no classes over the weekend, I hadn't seen Dave for two days. Even though we only spoke the one time, my heart quivered with the thought of seeing him again. The pleasant temperature and sunny blue sky on this Monday morning seem to predict today will be a great day. After taking extra care with my appearance, I did a final check of my reflection in my bedroom mirror. All the effort used to smooth my hair into a chic French braid was paying off.

Chin up, standing tall, I swipe my dreamy smile with pink lip gloss.

Wearing a new bright-yellow dress with matching wedges, I take my usual route to class. The big round clock on the tower at the end of the grassy knoll verifies I'm right on time. Slowing my pace, I scan the area for Dave. His friends are gathered under the big oak tree where they usually meet, but he's not with them. Maybe he's running late again? I smile, remembering our first meeting.

I want to get a glimpse of him without being obvious. My yellow dress is a poor camouflage against the green grass, gray sidewalks, and brown brick buildings. One of his friends nods my way, but his focus shifts back to the group. My face burns at being discovered, but I continue to meander down the sidewalk, darting glances around the quad in search of Dave.

The hammer on the large tower clock gongs. I'll be late for class if I wait any longer. My heart sinks. Chin tucked, I pick up my pace. Once seated in class, I try to pay attention to the lecture, but my mind hears *blah, blah, blah* as the teacher drones on. Instead of taking notes, I doodle a picture of a field of wilted sunflowers.

Tuesday, Wednesday, and Thursday are the same. Dave's absence convinces me he's not interested anymore. Maybe he never was?

Feeling stupid, I admonish myself, then revert to my old, dull routine—eat, class, eat, study, eat, sleep, repeat. The wake-up call from wishful thinking has me storing my dresses in the back of the closet where they belong.

Friday morning, the fall rains begin. Gray skies mirror my mood as I trek across campus. Heavy drops plop off the oversized black raincoat I borrowed from my dad's closet. The hood hides most of my face. I try to avoid the puddles that have formed in the cracks of the sidewalk, unsure whether my blue galoshes are waterproof or made purely for fashion. Either way, I regret not buying the matching raincoat now. Dad's raincoat is reminiscent of the ones sea captains wear in movies when the boat is about to capsize in torrential rain and large ocean swells.

Eyes down, I giggle at the mental image of me as a sea captain. The clock tower gongs. The building where my class is held is close. I'm ready to get out of the miserable cold, wet weather.

"Hey, is that you, Late?" a voice yells out as my feet cross the sidewalk by the oak tree.

I jerk my head up, unsure if I heard correctly under the hood of my raincoat. A few feet in front of me, Dave fights with a large umbrella covered with multicolored polka dots. The wind pulls at it, turning it inside out. In his other hand, he holds a large soggy poster board. His face lights up when our eyes meet. His mouth curls into one of his irresistible smiles. He drops the umbrella and points to the rain-streaked black letters on the sign—smeared but still readable: "Will you go out with me?"

I give him a bright smile. "Yes, yes, yes!"

After that, we were inseparable. Dave was a junior majoring in business and marketing. I was a sophomore studying journalism. He lived in the dorm. I lived with my dad a few blocks off campus. He was the youngest of five siblings. I was an only child. He came from Texas on a football scholarship. I came from Missouri with an academic scholarship. While we were as opposite as night and day, our differences didn't matter. We loved spending almost every waking moment together. Everything was perfect ... until it wasn't.

# CHAPTER TWENTY-FIVE

Present

"We're here." Tom jolts me back to the present as he pulls into a white chat parking lot. He finds a parking spot big enough to accommodate his tow truck and our rental. The small diner has azure siding with white shingles framing the windows. Five cedar picnic tables sit on the gravel.

We climb up the few steps to the entrance. I imagine we look like a trio of vagabonds as we search for a table. Our only option is a beige upholstered booth. The six brown leather barstools at the white Formica bar are occupied, so Delores heads for the empty booth.

The cement floor is painted beige and matches the walls. While the furnishing, flooring, and walls seem colorless, the farmhouse décor stands out. All three booths are topped with red-and-black checkered tablecloths. White handmade crocheted curtains hang from the three large windows, while two enormous hand-painted murals of chickens in barnyards adorn the beige concrete walls.

Above the cook's large black grill hangs a handwritten sign: "Sam and Hazel's Diner—we serve gluten and deep fry everything."

"Hello, Hazel." Tom waves to a woman serving the people in the booth next to ours. She wears a light-blue short-sleeved button-up polyester dress, a pressed white apron with front pockets, and white non-slip shoes. Her silver hair is teased high in an updo. Once her hands are empty, she waves back at Tom.

"Give me a minute. I'll be right back." She winks, then darts a quick glance at Delores and me before reaching the counter.

Hazel returns with silverware, napkins, and paper menus.

"These ladies had to be towed into town. Ran out of gas," Tom tells her.

"The poor dears." Hazel's lips form a sad pout.

I mentally roll my eyes, then berate myself for my bad attitude. I should be grateful I'm sitting in this booth instead of in a hot car in the middle of nowhere. I'm exhausted.

Delores points to the special written on a chalkboard hanging behind her: "Salmon and Roasted Potatoes." Delores and I order pancakes and bacon.

Tom asks for a loaded omelet.

Hazel jots down our orders on her notepad, then, looking straight at me, she scrunches her nose. "You may want to freshen up." She points to the women's restroom on the opposite side of the diner.

Delores belts out a laugh, drawing the other customers' attention. I cringe, remembering my reflection in the rearview mirror earlier. Delores rustles in her handbag, then hands me a stick of deodorant and a travel-sized bottle of perfume. What doesn't she have in that bag? I'm sure I stink after a long sweaty night in the car. Leaving the booth to visit the restroom, I walk with my head lowered, feeling several pairs of eyes boring into my back.

Once inside the small area, I let out a long sigh. My hunched shoulders relax, releasing the tension of the past twenty-four hours. I wet a paper towel and squirt some liquid soap from the dispenser, then vigorously scrub my armpits and the back of my neck. I cup more cool water in my hands and splash it on my face, then rub away the smeared mascara under my eyes. My hair is no longer straight, so I grab handfuls of water to douse the strands. I twist my frizzy, wet hair into a knot like I've often seen Emma do, binding the auburn mess into a bun on top of my head with a rubber band someone left on the vanity. I know it's gross, but anything's better than resembling a bushy-headed alpaca. A few sprigs of hair escape the bun, but I like the way they frame my face. My hairdo isn't salon worthy, but I am so much cooler with it pulled off my neck.

With a swipe of the deodorant stick under each armpit and a spritz of perfume on my neck and wrists, I leave the restroom, hoping I look better than when I entered.

In the corner of the diner, a few feet from me, sits an old jukebox. It's similar to the one at our local diner when I was a kid. Grandma would take me there for special occasions. We loved their milkshakes and ice cream sundaes. Wondering whether this one works, I stroll over to it. The semicircle tube on the top of the jukebox isn't flashing multi colors of light anymore, but a yellowed light illuminates several forty-five records beneath the glass.

I run my fingers across the worn selection buttons, reminiscing. "Please, can I have a quarter?" I hear my younger self beg Grandma.

"Just one," she'd say and wink at me. Then she would pull

out her perfumed handkerchief with the cross-stitched pink roses from her handbag and unfold it, revealing a quarter-and-a-half stick of Doublemint chewing gum tucked inside.

"For you, Grandma," I whisper, putting two quarters in the change slot. After scanning the list of songs, I push B6—"Kiss an Angel Good Morning" by Charlie Pride, one of my grandma's favorites.

Delores and Tom are cackling when I return to the table.

I sit back down and ask, "What are you two laughing about?"

"Oh, nothing." Delores's lips form a conspiratorial smile.

Tom winks at her, then changes the subject. "Good choice of song."

"Mm-hmm." I look back and forth between them. The vibe changed while I was freshening up. I sense some flirting going on.

Hazel brings our food. My mouth waters at the sight of the pancakes smothered with butter and maple syrup. Out of politeness, I wait for Hazel to leave the table before diving in, but she doesn't. Instead, she studies Delores and me. I want to tell her I cleaned up the best I could, but I refrain.

Oblivious to Hazel's presence, Delores and Tom continue to make googly eyes at each other.

I smile at Hazel, waiting for her to say something. She returns a halfhearted smile, then walks behind the counter and stares at a tiny black-and-white TV.

Sam, her husband and co-owner, joins her. She points at something on the screen and waves her arms while she talks. Sam nods. I squint to see what they are looking at, but the screen's too small to make out anything from this distance. She points again, then whispers something in Sam's ear. They both turn from the TV and gawk at me. Sam's eyes narrow.

Warning sirens blare in my head.

"Tom, I'm afraid we need to get going." I interrupt him mid-sentence.

Tom gives me a perturbed look, and Delores frowns at me.

"We need our car unhitched now. Could you gas it up too?" my voice commands, every muscle in my neck taut.

Tom rises, throwing his napkin onto his plate, then leaves our table and walks outside.

"What's the hurry, Sarah?" Delores asks in a surly tone.

Trying not to draw Hazel's and Sam's attention, I nod my head their direction. "They keep staring at us," I whisper.

"Who?" she blasts.

I cup my hand over the side of my mouth. "Sam and Hazel. But don't look."

Delores turns sideways to peek at them. She shoves my shoulder, then howls with laughter. "You've been in the desert too long. You're hallucinating." She snorts. "Hazel is busy cutting a pie, and Sam's cleaning the grill."

I glance their direction. She's right. Hazel and Sam focus on the tasks Delores described. Wincing, I poke a bite of my food and stuff it into my mouth. The uneasiness in the pit of my stomach remains.

When Tom returns to our table, I say, "Thank you," then hand him some cash from my billfold for the tow and gas.

Delores picks up their conversation from before.

Inwardly, I chide myself for being rude to Tom and indulging in my conspiracy theory. But then, from the corner of my eye, I notice Hazel watching us again. Goose bumps rise on my arms. My stomach rolls, threatening to eject the meal I just finished. I turn toward the counter, praying I'm wrong. I'm not. Hazel's menacing stare pierces me.

"That's it." I throw more cash onto the table for our food, and a generous tip, then grab Delores's arm and drag her from the booth. "Time to go."

Her mouth falls open. "What has gotten into you, Sarah?" Her eyes grow larger the more I pull her toward the door. "We haven't had our pie yet!"

Between clenched teeth, I say, "Take it to go."

"I haven't ordered any." She throws her hands up, releasing my grip on her arm. She walks over to Hazel, who's standing behind the counter. "Can I get a slice of that pie you're cutting, to go?" Sarcasm drips off the words "to go."

Hazel's eyes narrow as she looks from Delores to me. "Give me a minute to get a box." When she disappears into the back, Sam follows her.

I lean over the counter, hoping to overhear their conversation. There's a repeated swoosh, then a *click, click, click* with each turn of a rotary phone. I know that sound because my grandma had a rotary phone in her house.

"What's the last number, Sam?" Tension fills Hazel's voice.

"Six," he answers, then there's one last *swoosh, click, click, click*.

Seconds after the last click, Hazel begins talking in a hushed tone, making it difficult for me to understand what she's saying. The person on the other end of the line must be having trouble hearing her, too, because her voice grows louder.

I concentrate, trying my best to listen to her end of the conversation over Delores's humming next to me.

"Yes, she said her name is Delores. She looks like the photo on the TV. I'm not sure what the other woman's name is, but she kind of looks like the other lady pictured, just … messier."

I exhale, not aware I've been holding my breath. I grip the counter until the room quits spinning. Who is Hazel talking to? What photo is she referring to? We are in the middle of nowhere. Who knows what these people are into.

The humming beside me has stopped. I glance to see

Delores is no longer beside me. She has returned to the booth with Tom and three pieces of pie. I guess she grew tired of waiting.

I march over and grab her plate of pie. "It's time to tell Tom goodbye. You can take your pie with you," I say. The plate shakes from my trembling hands.

"I guess we need to go now. It was nice meeting you, Tom." She waves at him, then turns a scowl on me.

"What has gotten into you?" she asks again when we're outside. "Your face is white as a sheet."

"I'll fill you in once we're on the road and far away from here." I race to the rental.

# CHAPTER TWENTY-SIX

Delores pooh-poohs me when I describe the suspicious behavior of the diner's owners, so I give up trying to convince her. My spooky vibe changes to dread as I watch the blue dot on my cell map move closer to the address from the back of the photo.

Numbers painted on a black mailbox protruding from the side of the road at the end of a driveway match our destination. Back in the driver's seat, I turn the car slowly into the dirt driveway. Grass and weeds intertwine with gray rock. The small house appears deserted, except for the rottweiler mix chained to a tree, growling and baring its teeth. No ribs show along his sides. His belly is plump from eating well.

Red concrete steps lead to a screened-in porch. Chipped paint and broken lap siding expose patches of gray-and-black tar paper. The house is in desperate need of repair. A rosebush pushes upward at the corner of the porch, the yellow blooms struggling to be seen amongst the weeds and tall grass threatening to strangle the bush.

My stomach lurches, and bile rises in my throat. My chest

sinks from an invisible weight threatening to crush my lungs. My foot aches from pushing on the brake. My hand is unwilling to shift the car into park. The impulse to switch the car from drive to reverse overwhelms me, then Delores's palm covers my knuckles. I give her a weak smile.

"You don't have to go in, you know," she says, once again reading my thoughts. "Judging from the state of the house, no one may live here anymore." She pats my hand, calming my nerves.

My breath catches in my chest. Needing an ounce of Delores's courage, I ask with a shaky voice, "Will you go in with me?"

"Absolutely." Her agreement holds no hesitation.

Lightheaded from holding my breath, I release a loud exhale, then suck in more air—one, two, three, four. I shift the car into park and turn off the ignition. The whir of the engine stops, and my thoughts grow even louder.

Delores opens her door first, exits, then walks to the front of the SUV and waits. Pulling down the car visor, I check my reflection in the mirror. Burning eyes—threatening tears— stare back at me. I squeeze them shut. What am I doing here?

Outside, a muffled, "Are you coming, Sarah?" breaks through the chattering in my brain.

"Yes," I mutter. After wiping my sweaty palms on my jeans, I exit the car and join Delores.

The sidewalk to the house is cracked and uneven. I glance at the dog, praying his chain holds. His growling has ramped up to incessant, deep barking. Delores and I quicken our steps. The screen door to the porch is unlatched. It creaks when we open it. A few more steps and we stand at the entrance to the house. I gently rap on the splintered wooden door. No one responds. Gathering my courage, I knock louder.

"Just a minute," a woman inside yells. "Hold your horses."

Delores and I wait as instructed. To keep from passing out, I take a big breath in, hold, silently count to four, then exhale. A deadbolt clicks just as I take in another breath. A woosh of air escapes my lips as I nervously anticipate meeting the person inside. A chain lock restrains the door from swinging wide. Through a small opening, two hazel eyes behind overly large frames stare back at us. "Whatever you're selling, I don't want any," the woman growls. She raises her voice, sounding agitated. "And don't give me any of those religious tracks, either."

Delores glances at me, wide-eyed, some of her bright-red lipstick chewed off. She looks as nervous as I feel but returns her gaze to the door. "Ma'am, my friend here found a photo with your address on the back. We were wondering if we could ask you a few questions about the mother of the little girl in this picture. We thought you might be related. Her married name was Phoebe Hayes." Delores slips the black-and-white photo through the small opening.

The woman studies the photo, then turns it over. "She's dead." Her gravelly voice holds no emotion. "If she owes you money, I can't help you," she adds in a harsh tone.

The impulse to run as fast as my legs can carry me and forget this whole thing tears at me.

Before she can close the door in our faces, words rush from Delores's mouth. "Yes, we know that, ma'am. My friend here" —she points at me—"is her daughter. She has driven a very long way to ask you a few simple questions. I promise we won't take much of your time."

The woman pulls her bifocals up so that her eyes appear larger as they move from my face to my toes, inspecting every inch of me.

Embarrassed and a little irritated, I find my voice again.

"Like my friend said, I promise this will only take a few minutes."

The door slams closed, then a clash of the chain lock hits the wood. The door swings open, revealing the woman in a tattered faded-pink bathrobe. Streaks of silver intertwined with short auburn hair hang lifeless around her face. Even though she's small, she terrifying. With her arms positioned on her hips, she narrows her eyes at me and turns her frown into a full-blown scowl. She swivels her back to us, saying nothing, and walks out of view. Delores and I shrug at each other and follow, entering her home.

Standing in her living room, we watch her cross over to a worn brown recliner and take a seat. She motions to a small loveseat.

A curled-up tabby cat and her kittens sleep on a full-sized couch, undisturbed by our presence. A black cat bats at a dusty ball of yarn on a threadbare ottoman. The only space not occupied by cats is the loveseat.

Delores swipes the fabric with her hand, removing some of the multicolored cat hair, before taking her seat. I scrunch in beside her.

My eyes wander the living room, taking in the gray fur ball tiptoeing on top of the box TV with rabbit ears. In the bay window, an enormous calico curls on the ledge, sunning itself. I hear another cat's loud meows from a nearby room. Remembering my manners, I return my gaze to the woman in the recliner, who stares back at me. I clear my throat. "I'm Sarah, and this is Delores."

"I'm Maeve," she states in a gruff tone.

I reach for my lip balm in my purse, hoping to escape her probing eyes. My lips burn from biting them.

"You look a lot like her, you know," Maeve says.

My head pops up from digging for the small tube in the

mess of tissues, receipts, and ink pens. "No, I didn't know that."

"You do." Her gaze rests on my face, softening as she adds, "Especially around your eyes."

"I know so little about my mom." My voice quivers. "What can you tell me about her?"

Mauve hesitates a moment, then says, "We were sisters. I'm your aunt."

My mouth gapes open. I feel like a bomb just dropped on me. Why didn't I know my mom had a sister?

"I didn't always look like this." She gives me a bitter smile and removes her glasses. "At one time, people considered me pretty."

"That's not what I was thinking at all," I say emphatically. "I'm surprised no one ever mentioned I have an aunt. Are there more siblings? More family?" My head throbs as I hold back impending tears at the possibility.

"No, it was just me and your mom growing up." She picks up a lighter and a pack of cigarettes from the TV tray next to her.

Frowning, I wait for her to continue.

She smacks the cigarette pack into the palm of her hand until a long, thin rolled cigarette escapes its confinement. Mauve lights the end, then takes a slow draw. The tip smolders and shrinks. After a beat, she exhales the smoke. "Your mom, Phoebe, had big, unattainable dreams. She chased one after another, searching for fame and fortune until the day she died." Mauve sucks in another drag from her cigarette, then puffs out more billowing smoke. A whitish-gray cloud of vapor rises to the yellow-stained ceiling.

She smashes the cigarette in an overfull ashtray and grabs a large magnifying glass, also lying on the TV tray. Moving the beveled glass across the photo, she begins her monologue again. "Looking at the date on this picture, your parents took this trip right before she ran off to Hollywood. She wrote me a letter when you all returned home with a few details about the trip, then added she had big news to tell me. I didn't hear from her again for months—not until she came knocking on my door, tail between her legs like some scraggly mutt."

"She said she'd been to California. Some man in a suit and a big silver Buick approached her in the parking lot of your town's grocery store. He told her he was a talent agent and promised that with her good looks, she was guaranteed a lead in a movie. Phoebe, always wide-eyed and naïve, left with him right then and there, leaving you and your dad behind. After that turned out to be a bust, she went back to your dad, but of course she got a wild hair again. The last time Phoebe took off, your dad told her not to come back."

Heartsick, I ask, "When she came to visit you, did she ever talk about me?"

"Not that I recall," Mauve says flatly.

My heart shatters into pieces.

"But we lost touch years before she died. I knew she had a little girl, but nothing more."

I look at my hands so she can't see the hot tears building behind my eyes.

"You know, I never met your father. Was he nice?"

Before I have time to answer, she jumps up from her recliner, "Oh, I almost forgot. Your mother mailed me a shoebox not long before she passed. I had no idea why, or even what I was supposed to do with it, so it's been sitting in the bottom of my closet for years." Mauve's tone is matter-of-fact. "I never looked inside it. Knowing Phoebe, it's probably a bunch of junk, but you might as well have it." She shrugs and then goes to retrieve it.

Tied in knots, I'm unsure if I should be happy to have

something of my mom's or disappointed her only possession is a shoebox full of junk.

Delores and I wait for Mauve in silence. I'm too fragile and shaken to talk. After several minutes, she returns and hands me a yellowed, decomposing shoebox with "Phoebe" written in bold red letters on the top.

Delores and I stand to leave. Hugging the box to my chest, I say in a tearful voice, "Thank you, Mauve. We've taken enough of your time."

She doesn't say anything more.

I turn to leave, but a burning in my chest stops me. I become hyper-focused on the walls around us. No pictures of children hang on the brown paneling, nor do family photos grace an end table. Compelled for a reason I can't explain, I ask, "Do you have kids?"

She frowns. "I have two kids, but we haven't talked in years," she says in a flat tone. "Phoebe and I had crappy childhoods. We left home as soon as we were old enough to take care of ourselves and never looked back. I wanted to do better by my kids, but I didn't know how. They left home as soon as they could, just like we did. Some say it's a generational curse and nothing can be done about it." She shrugs. "It is what it is."

I ponder her words and study her for a moment. Maeve is no longer gruff and scary. She appears small and frail with her head bent, trying to relight the remains of the cigarette she snuffed out earlier. Even though her circumstances are of her own making, my heart hurts for her. My aunt's gaze darts up as I walk over to her. The scowl she's had since we walked into her home has softened. Wet, lackluster eyes peer into mine. There are no creases around her mouth from smiling or laughing, only deep grooves around her eyes and forehead. She looks tired—worn out. The kind of worn out that comes from living a life without love or family. She doesn't get up, so I bend down, placing my arms around her shoulders to give her an awkward hug. I don't expect her to embrace me back, and she doesn't, but I know in my gut it's the right thing to do. Before releasing her, I place my face beside hers, wanting to store this moment in my memories. Wetness seeps around the corners of her eyes. I release her and nod, feeling her sadness ... and maybe regret?

Delores is waiting for me on the porch. Once I'm outside, we don't speak as we walk down the sidewalk, climb into the car, or drive down the highway. I'm grateful for the silence, needing time to process today before I can talk about it.

We drive until dark with no planned destination. It's late when Delores points to a motel sign posted on the highway. I nod. We take the exit, check in, and settle in for the night. Pajamas on and lights off, I lie on my side. Using the glow of the streetlight outside entering our window, I glance at Delores in the bed next to me. With my stomach tied in knots and not knowing what to make of the flood of contradictory emotions filling my heart, I ask, "Do you think my aunt is right?"

She doesn't respond. Maybe she's asleep.

I close my eyes, trying to drown out the negative thoughts banging around in my head.

"About what?" she asks.

A tear escapes the corner of my eye. "Am I under a generational curse?"

Delores sits up in the middle of her bed and shifts toward me. I can't see her face, only the outline of her body. "That's poppycock," she says, her voice filled with authority.

I can't help but grin at her choice of word.

"And furthermore, that's an excuse people use to not do better or be better than their folks," she adds. "Everyone has choices to make. Some may have a harder time rising above their circumstances, but when we become adults, it's time to act like adults."

"But Emma and me ..." My voice cracks.

"Don't let a bitter old woman make you doubt you're a good mom. Everything I know and have learned about you confirms that truth," she declares.

Grateful teardrops pepper the outer creases of my eyes, running down my temples and into my hair. "Thanks, Delores," I whisper.

She doesn't reply, but the creak of her bed tells me she has lain back down.

After a while, Delores's breathing deepens. She's curled her body into a fetal position and faces the wall closest to her. The shoebox Mauve gave me sits on the dresser, a muted outline in the darkness. Curious about what's inside yet dreading what I will find, I can't sleep.

Curiosity wins. I tiptoe to the dresser and bring the box back to the bed.

Delores hasn't moved and has her back to me, which builds my confidence. I've shared a lot with her, but opening this box is something I need to do on my own. I'm hoping the flashlight app on my now-charged phone won't wake her.

I carefully pull the tape away from the top, and the lid comes free. I turn the box upside down and spill old, yellowed newspaper clippings onto the bedspread. Thinking my mom used them to protect something valuable, I spread them out. There's nothing but old clippings. Junk, like Mauve said. Why did I expect more?

I wad one of the papers in my hand and pitch it into the box. I grab another clipping and another, wadding each one into a ball. Placing the shoebox a little farther on the bed, I shoot each wad like a basketball into a hoop. Angry at myself for letting hope in, adrenaline pumps through my chest with each shot. I throw a wad farther than I mean to. It ricochets off the side of the box and lands on the floor. With a huff, I point my cell toward the green-and-blue carpet. The beam of the flashlight lands on the fallen paper. When I bend to retrieve the wad, my eyes land on the word "Rivertown."

With a racing heart, I pick it up and smooth the paper flat. I scan the headline. "Riverview Eagles Win Against Ferndale Bulldogs." A picture of my volleyball team sits under the headline. Red ink circles sixteen-year-old me in my uniform.

Frantic, I smooth another clipping. This one reads, "Sarah Hayes Plans to Attend Missouri University Next Fall." I remember Dad sending my senior picture to *Rivertown Daily News* for this article.

My heart threatens to beat out of my chest as I pick up each yellowed wad of paper. It takes restraint to carefully smooth each clipping and not tear them while hungry for more information. There's an announcement of my engagement to Dave attached to a clipping of our wedding photo. Had my mother been keeping up with me through our local paper all those years?

One last piece of paper remains. I take a moment to rein in my emotions before opening it. "Dave and Sarah Goodwin are the Proud Parents of Emma Goodwin, Born at the Riverview Memorial Hospital." A big red heart is drawn around it. Happy tears trickle down my face.

"Is everything okay?" Delores startles me.

"Yes." I swipe at my cheeks and sniffle. "I'm good."

As I place the lid on the shoebox, a life-changing thought surfaces.

In her own way, my mother loved me.

# CHAPTER TWENTY-SEVEN

After playing a game of Jenga with our luggage in the back hatch, Delores and I settle into our seats. We both stare ahead, not saying a word. Several moments pass. The car idles.

Delores finally breaks the silence to ask, "Where to next?"

"Home, I guess," I say flatly.

I turn to watch her reaction. She exhales a dramatic sigh. When I begin typing my home address into my map app, Delores asks another question.

"Didn't you say your daughter moved to Arizona?"

I stop punching in coordinates and glance at her.

"We could go see her," she says with a hopeful smile.

Struggling to process the last twenty-four hours, my emotions are like a roller coaster close to driving off the tracks. Continuing our trip to visit Emma seems like a bad idea. My face might betray the turmoil churning inside. Emma needs to see me at my best. My heart sinks as another thought collides with the ones already rattling around my head. Would she be happy to see me, or would she think I was intruding?

Delores must take my silence as a "no" because she sighs again. "Let's go home." The spark in her eyes is gone.

Not wanting to disappoint her, I say, "I don't know if I'm ready for our adventure to end."

"Atta girl." She slaps her knee with a satisfied grin.

"We can surprise her." I avert my eyes so she won't read my doubt.

I don't call ahead, fearful Emma will make up an excuse why now is not a good time to visit. Pain sears my heart as I recall the many times she has put me off in the past. I would plan weekend visits with her at college, but she would call me later to cancel. Something always seemed to come up on her end.

Delores moves the tuner on the radio while I pull onto the highway. The piano intro to Patsy Cline's iconic "Crazy" plays. This song was one of my dad's favorites. Delores turns up the volume. With her red manicured fingers, she grips an imaginary microphone, then joins Patsy on the first verse. When the chorus comes, she points at me to take over. Our duet fills the car. We giggle after our dramatic musical finale.

The silliness helps dissipate the heaviness in my heart. Delores has a way of making me feel lighter. That's the wonder of Delores. She turns bad situations around simply by being herself. Before I can tell her how much I appreciate her friendship, her cell phone chimes.

"Hello, Agnus. Did you girls make it home safely?" Delores asks.

I hear Agnus's panicked voice on the other end but can't make out what she's saying.

"Slow down! You're talking too fast." Delores listens for a minute or two, then yells into the phone, "You've gotta be kidding me."

Taking my eyes off the road momentarily, I glance at

Delores. Her eyes are as big as saucers, and her face is beet red. My stomach drops as a range of emotions crosses her face.

Before I have time to ask if I need to pull over, red-and-blue lights flash in my rearview mirror. Our vehicle is the only one on the highway. The cop car accelerates, shortening the distance between us. The speedometer indicates I'm only driving two miles over the speed limit.

"I'm so sorry, Sarah." Delores's face is now drained of color. "You better pull over."

With a hammering heart, I flip the right blinker on and brake until our speed slows enough to steer the car onto the shoulder.

In the rearview mirror, I watch as the police officer exits his car in a brown uniform with a wide-brimmed hat. He looks young—maybe early twenties? He walks cautiously toward the back of our SUV, gripping his holstered gun with his right hand.

"Slowly get out of the car with your hands above your heads," he instructs.

Delores mumbles something under her breath, but I can't make it out.

We glance at each other, then unbuckle our seat belts. Once we've opened our doors, we slide at a snail's pace out of our seats and stand next to the car. A large lump in my throat makes it impossible to speak. It's my heart.

"Hands above your heads," the officer yells again.

Wary, I do as I'm told. Delores does not.

"There's been a big misunderstanding." She strides toward the officer.

He spreads his legs in a wide stance and holds his palms out, signaling her to stop. Thankfully, she does. "Are you Delores Wright?" he asks.

She nods.

He walks closer to her, his right hand back on his gun. With his left hand, he pulls out his phone and shows Delores the screen.

My arms ache from holding them in the air. I begin to lower them, but the officer's eyes dart my way, nailing me in place. With my temples pounding and my arms throbbing, discomfort overrides my fear. "What is going on?"

Delores turns to me, red-faced again. "Someone put out a Silver Alert on me when I didn't return home with the tour group." Her nostrils flare. "They think you kidnapped me."

"What?" My mouth gapes open.

The officer walks closer to me. Keeping a safe distance, he pans his phone close enough for me to see an atrocious picture of myself. Someone at the diner Tom towed us to must have snapped the photo. It reminds me of those terrible paparazzi photos of celebrities at their worst that gossip magazines use. My frizzy auburn hair is tied in a knot on top of my head. I'm wearing a crumpled, sweat-stained white linen shirt with denim shorts. There's not a speck of makeup on my face. To add insult to injury, I'm listed as Delores Wright's kidnapper under the photo.

"You can lower your arms now," the officer says. "But put them behind your back."

I gulp, my mind racing.

He walks behind me and locks handcuffs onto my wrists. "I'm placing you under arrest for the kidnapping of Delores Wright. You have the right to remain silent. Anything you say can and will be used against you in a court of law. You have the right to an attorney. If you can't afford an attorney, one will be provided for you. Do you understand the rights I have just read you?"

My legs threaten to buckle under me.

"Release her now," Delores shouts. "She's not a kidnapper.

Who reported me missing?" she asks through clenched teeth. When the police officer doesn't respond, she shouts in his face. "Let her go!"

His cheeks redden.

If she doesn't calm down, we'll be sharing a jail cell.

Her eyes widen. "My kids did this, didn't they? What did they tell you? I'm incompetent? I can prove I'm not. Ask me anything." Her lips curl as she tightens her jaw. "My full name is Delores Annabelle Wright. I live at 200 Right Street in Ferndale, Missouri. I was born June twelfth, 1954." She huffs. "Who's the president? Joe Biden. What year is it? Twenty twenty-four. What else do you need to know?" She is again dangerously close to his face.

The officer gives me a suspicious glare, then releases his hold on my cuffs and pulls a little black notebook from his back pocket. He opens it, flipping through the pages until he lands on the one he's searching for. Pointing to the handwriting scribbled on the page, he says, "Your car matches the make, model, color, and license plate number. You both match the physical descriptions of the abductor and abductee." With a flick of his wrist, he flips the notebook closed.

Exasperated, I growl. "Because we are those people, but no one has been kidnapped."

"We're traveling together. I'm with Sarah of my own free will. Why won't you listen?" Her voice rises.

The officer removes his wide-brimmed hat, revealing cropped black hair damp from sweat. "Listen, this is my first day on the job. I'm going to have to take you both in." He enunciates each word in a slow, soft tone like we are children unable to grasp the situation. "I'll let the sheriff sort this all out."

Delores glances at me, a pained look in her eyes. "Can you at least take her out of the handcuffs?"

"I'm afraid not." He points to his car. "I'll need you to sit in the front seat with me. She"—he takes me by the shoulders—"will ride in the back."

"Do you trust me to get our purses and lock the car?" Delores chides.

The officer gives a curt nod, then ushers me to the police car. He grips my shoulders the whole way as if he expects me to run at any moment. Where would I even go? Once we reach the car, he places his hand on my head to guide me into the back seat.

My face flames, but not from the heat. I grit my teeth but remain silent.

Delores shuffles to the passenger side of the patrol car, weighed down by the oversized bag she calls a purse and my handbag. A ringtone sounds inside my bag, but I can't answer it. Has Dave or Emma seen the Silver Alert with my picture?

"Can Delores answer that?" I yell from the back seat.

The officer hesitates, then looks pointedly at her. "Sure, but no funny business."

She digs in my purse, then pulls out my cell. She taps the answer button and puts the call on speaker.

"Sarah?" Dave's voice is panicked.

"Hi, Dave," Delores says.

"Who is this?" he asks, sounding confused.

"I'm Delores, Sarah's friend," she says cheerfully.

"Okaaaay." He pauses for several seconds, probably trying to piece together why someone other than me answered my phone. "Can I talk to Sarah?" His voice is tense. He's trying to be polite, but he's about to lose his composure.

"She can't talk right now," Delores says. "She's a little busy being arrested. I wasn't allowed to sit in the back of the police car with her, so there's this wire barrier between us." She shoots the officer a disapproving glower. "No need to worry, though. I'll be sure to remind her to call you once we're out of jail."

"Delores," I yell, alarmed she's frightening Dave.

The officer glances at her and makes a circular motion with his right hand and index finger. "Well, Dave, it's been nice talking to you, but the police officer wants me to wrap up this conversation. I'll be sure to have Sarah call you once we reach the police station. It's still procedure to get one phone call, right?" She glances at the officer for confirmation. He gives an impatient nod while keeping his eyes on the road. "Yep, he said that's still the law."

He opens his palm, motioning Delores to hand him the phone. Instead, she hits the end call button, cutting Dave off mid-sentence. She tucks the phone back in my purse, then places her hands on her lap. In the rearview mirror, I watch the officer huff in irritation.

My thoughts spin, imagining horrible scenarios that must be playing through Dave's head. My cell rings again, but we all ignore it this time.

# CHAPTER TWENTY-EIGHT

My wrists hurt from the cuffs pinning my arms behind my back. Heat flushes my face again. I'm so mad I could spit nails.

"Dispatch, this is Officer Luther Barlowe. I have the kidnapper in custody." The officer grips a radio handset in his right hand. Static follows, then a loud click.

"Do you need assistance?" a female voice asks.

Officer Barlowe gives Delores a questioning look. She shakes her head. He stares at me in his rearview mirror. I drop my chin to my chest, lowering my eyes to my lap.

There's more static and another click. "No, I'm good. We're twenty miles from the sheriff's office. Let Sheriff Emmitt know we're coming."

"Will do," the woman says. There's more static, ending with another click.

Delores keeps her hands on her lap. She's quiet as she watches out the passenger window. My chest burns from the massive amounts of adrenaline pulsing through my veins. The only thing keeping me from a full-on panic attack is the sporadic crackle of the radio reporting other incidents in the area. I would chuckle at the ridiculous situations shared over the police airwaves if I wasn't so upset.

"Can an officer go out to Mary Bloom's place? She said she can't leave her house because a squirrel is terrorizing her porch."

There's a pause, a click, and more static. "I've got it," a male officer replies.

"Oh wait, we just got a call from Suzie's Grocery Mart. A suspicious item is in the vegetable bin," the dispatcher says. "Can you check on that first?"

"I'm outside the grocery mart now," the male officer replies again.

"Proceed with caution," the dispatcher says.

After a good ten minutes, there's a click, static, and another click. "I evacuated the store, but it was a false alarm. I guess a kiwano was put in the shipment of produce this week."

"What's a kiwano?" the dispatcher asks between clicks and static.

"I'm not sure, but it's orange and spiky. It's downright ugggly," he says. "It looked like some kind of mutant sea urchin. I was going to touch it, but it moved, so I shot it. Sticky orange goo exploded everywhere. It was a mess. Once we calmed down, Suzie and I googled it. It's some kind of exotic fruit-vegetable thing. Anyway, everyone is safe." He pauses, then clears his throat. "Tell Sh-sh-sheriff Emmitt the d-department owes S-s-suzie a new produce bin." Static. Click.

How proud Officer Barlowe must feel compared to his comrade. Apprehending a kidnapper sets him apart from the squirrel-hunting, fruit-shooting officer.

The highway we're driving on runs straight through the town of Martinville—population six hundred and nine—and our destination. Officer Barlowe slows the car to a crawl, giving me time to survey the town. A few brown brick buildings line both sides of the street. The first building we pass has a large hand-drawn sign displayed above its double doors: "Suzie's Grocery Mart." An officer wearing the same uniform as Luther stands in the center of a small group of people huddled in the parking lot, his head bowed as he writes in a little black notebook.

Next to the grocery mart is a two-pump gas station. The gas pumps have large bulbous tops attached to red-and-white tanks, reminding me of ones I've seen in old black-and-white movies. As we pass by, a loud *ding* sounds when a car drives into the gas station parking lot. An elderly man in navy-blue cotton coveralls scurries out to meet the car. Instead of getting out, the driver waits behind the steering wheel. The gas attendant pulls the black hose with the silver nozzle from the pump, then disappears to the other side. Numbers flip at a turtle's pace, displaying the gallons transferring from the antiquated pump to the car.

Mesmerized by the feeling of traveling back in time, I don't realize we've stopped in the designated patrol car parking spot right away.

Before Officer Barlowe shuts off the ignition, Delores throws open her door, jumps from her seat, and bolts out of the car. She makes a beeline for the brown wooden door with the sign hanging above it that reads: "Martinville Sherriff's Office."

Officer Barlowe yanks open his door, lunging out of the police car toward the sidewalk. "Stop!" he shouts, his hand on his holster.

Delores freezes in place like she's playing the children's game Statue, her stride paused in an awkward position.

Officer Barlowe groans, then backs up, never taking his eyes off Delores. He opens my door and pulls me from the car.

With a firm grip, he holds onto my cuffed wrists and marches me down the sidewalk to the entrance of the small building. Music blares from a nearby vehicle. Unthinking, I twist around to look. The driver ogles me, pointing a finger as his car passes. Cringing, I spin back around, lowering my eyes to focus on my feet. I jerk my head up when I hear a loud gasp. A few feet in front of me, a young woman pushing a baby stroller halts. She stares at the cuffs on my wrists, then her eyes rise to meet mine.

Without warning, she runs into the street, pushing the baby stroller with force. A car's brakes screech. Smoke rises from the skid marks left on the asphalt. The young woman screams, and the driver sticks his head out the window. "Watch where you're walking, lady!"

The woman doesn't move but shifts her glower to me. The driver honks at her. She quickly pushes the stroller to the other side of the road, and the wheels bounce when they hit the concrete sidewalk.

"Don't mind her." Delores huffs and shakes her head.

We walk the remaining steps to the sheriff's building. Nausea hits my stomach full force. *Please don't throw up now.*

Officer Barlowe motions to Delores. She rolls her eyes, then grips the metal handle, pulling the door open. She holds it while Officer Barlowe shoves me inside.

A burly man with a badge stands in a tiny waiting area. He wears the same uniform but without the hat. He has a full head of wavy gray hair. His narrowed blue-gray eyes study first Delores, then shift to me. A new cluster of flames rises from my neck into my face. Even the roots of my hair seem to be on fire. Hot, angry tears threaten. I want to swipe my hand at my eyes before tears of embarrassment fall, but the cuffs don't allow it. The sheriff's gaze softens. He instructs the arresting officer to sit me in a nearby chair. "I think it's okay to take her cuffs off, Luther, but keep an eye on her."

Luther unlocks the cuffs. He moves away from me like I might bite him, then stands between me and the exit, his wary eyes never leaving me.

"Are you the man in charge? Sheriff Caddel?" Delores points to his name tag.

"So they say." He ignores her irate tone and gives her a courteous smile, then extends his beefy hand. She places her dainty one in his. His large palm swallows her hand, rings and all. "Most people call me Emmitt," he says, then releases her. "I have a few questions for you, if you don't mind." His voice is as smooth as honey. "Follow me." He points to an office door.

Delores glances over her shoulder at me. I nod, sending her an unspoken message. I'll be fine. She gives me a rueful smile, then follows Sheriff Emmitt into his office. He closes the door.

A big analog clock hangs on the wall above Officer Luther. I wish I'd worn my watch. Every time I peek at the clock, I'm met with his unblinking stare. It feels like an eternity has passed since Delores and the sheriff left me out here, but finally, the office door opens. Delores and the sheriff emerge laughing. Their relaxed postures and jovial smiles give the impression they're longtime friends.

"You might want to call your kids and let them know you're fine, Delores," Sheriff Emmitt tells her.

She scowls at him.

"Or I can if you don't want to talk to them." He shrugs. "It's up to you, but it might be time you have a conversation with them. It sounds like it's long overdue."

"I'll handle it." She sighs and presses her red lips into a grim line.

His eyes move from her face to mine. "I'm sorry for the handcuffs, ma'am. This isn't our protocol for this kind of situation, but Luther's new. I hate to put him on probation, being we're shorthanded, but I will if you think it's warranted. He's really a good guy."

I glance over at Luther, who holds his hat between his lowered hands. His gaze drops to the floor.

My anger and embarrassment dissolve into compassion. At his downturned face, I remind myself it's his first day on the job and he's just a kid. About the same age as Emma. "It's okay," I say. "No harm done. Besides, he gave me an entertaining story to tell my husband." I titter, then sober. "If Dave doesn't kill me first."

Sheriff Emmitt's wide smile fades to a worried frown.

My face bursts into flames again. "Just joking. No killing, I promise."

Delores blasts out a laugh. "She's such a joker."

His shoulders relax and he lets out a low chuckle.

Delores looks pointedly at me.

"You ladies won't get any more trouble from us. I'll be sure to take your names off the Silver Alert too," the sheriff assures us. His cheeks crinkle around his eyes when he grins this time.

I nod, wanting to smile back, but my mouth refuses. The thought of leaving this office, this town, and this nightmare behind has me jumping to my feet. I channel all my willpower to keep from running out the door. Instead, I calmly walk toward the exit. My hand is inches from the metal door handle leading us to freedom. Then I remember our rental is several miles away. A sigh escapes my mouth loud enough for everyone in the lobby to hear.

Shutting my eyes tight, I whirl around and bump straight into Luther. Delores giggles. I narrow my eyes and shoot daggers at her. She smirks. Luther's face flushes. He takes a step back.

"Sorry, ma'am. I'll take you to your car." He must have

realized my predicament. He skirts around Delores and me to hold the door open. We walk outside. Several townspeople still gathered in the grocery store parking lot pivot to gawk at us.

I'm positive the topic of conversation is my incarceration. "This time I'm riding in front," I declare in a booming voice.

"I've always wanted to ride in the back of a cop car," Delores says from behind us.

I shake my head.

Luther exceeds the speed limit by a good twenty miles per hour. Is he as ready to be rid of us as we are to be rid of him? Delores tries to engage him in a conversation, asking questions about his family and job, but he only answers with a curt "yes" or "no." White-knuckling the steering wheel all the way back to our rental, he keeps his eyes focused on the road.

Finally, a gleam of silver flashes under the bright sunlight. Luther and I exhale sighs of relief in unison.

As soon as he comes to a complete stop, I jump out of the cop car, ready to sprint to the SUV.

"I can't get out," Delores yells from the back. Luther springs from his seat and opens her door. "Sorry, about that, ma'am. It automatically locks to keep criminals from escaping." He gives her an apologetic smile.

She pats his cheek. "You're a good boy, Luther. Don't be so hard on yourself."

His face turns crimson. Luther slides back into the driver's seat but doesn't drive away until we're buckled in our rental and our engine gives a low, steady purr.

The steering wheel scorches my fingers, making it too hot to hold onto and drive. I let the car idle, waiting for the warm air pushing out from the vents to blow cold.

Ecstatic to be out of trouble and back in our rental, I only now notice Delores's downturned face.

"What's wrong?" I ask.

A big teardrop plops on her lap. What's happening to my bubbly, nothing-bothers-me friend?

"Oh, Sarah, I'm so sorry for getting you into this mess. My kids are overprotective of me. If I'd known they would pull something like this, I wouldn't have come along." Her bangles clang against each other when she covers her eyes with her hands. She jerks the bangles off and throws them onto the floorboard, then swipes at her face.

"It's okay, really," I say. "Like I told the sheriff, it will make a funny story when I get past the embarrassment." I laugh for the first time today.

She lifts her head. Her brilliant blue eyes are no longer filled with mischief and fun. They're lackluster. For the first time since starting this trip, she looks tired. Or is she discouraged?

Taking her hand in mine, I say in a slow, reassuring tone, "I'm okay. Everything's fine. It's a blessing to have kids who are worried and looking out for you."

She sniffs and wipes at her nose with her free hand. Then her eyes soften, and she gives me a grateful smile.

"Besides, when you were trying your best to prove your mental competence to the rookie, I learned something new about you."

"What's that?" The mischievous glint returns to her eyes.

Tilting my head, I say in a singsong voice, "Today is your birthday." I grin. "We need to celebrate. Where would you like to go?"

Her face lights up. "How far is Vegas?"

# CHAPTER TWENTY-NINE

After a quick phone call to assure a baffled Dave that I'm fine, I type Las Vegas into the map search bar. Three routes pop up on the tiny screen. None of them are a direct shot.

"It seems there's no easy way to get to Vegas from here." I show Delores the routes highlighted on my cell. "The quickest route has us crossing over a few small highways, then onto Interstate Fifteen. We should make it by the end of the day." I raise my eyes from the phone to her face. We exchange smiles.

"Here we go." I shift the car into drive. The gravelly sound of the tires leaving the shoulder has me pressing harder on the accelerator.

Delores squeals. I chuckle. Her happier mood fills the car's cabin, raising my spirits too. The song "Viva Las Vegas" fills my head with anticipation of bright lights, shows, and food buffets.

Cruising at a faster speed limit than I'm used to, it doesn't take us long to reach the Highway 50 sign. Just past the sign on the right is a gas station. Even though the fuel gauge reads three-quarters full, I'm not taking any chances of being stranded on the road again.

While I gas up, Delores heads into the convenience store. It takes her a while to return. After hooking the nozzle back on the pump, I pull out my phone to review our route again. The sound of the back door opening draws my attention away from the map. A loud thud hits the floorboard. Curious, I open the back door on my side. Delores grunts when she tries to push two large paper bags between the two passenger seats and spills the contents all over the floorboard.

"Wow." I gape at the scattered beef jerky, licorice sticks, chips, peanut butter crackers, and canned sodas.

Delores laughs. "It's not a road trip if you don't make yourself sick stuffing your face along the way."

"So much for eating healthy." I pick up a bag of chips and open them.

Delores grabs another bag and a can of soda for each of us, then returns to her seat.

As I slide behind the wheel, a pop and fizz come from her side of the car. Once we're buckled in, we giggle like two teenage girls on a joyride. I put the SUV in reverse, clearing the gas pump, then shift into drive, returning my focus to the road.

Delores turns the knob on the radio left, then right. Nothing but static plays through the speakers. With a loud sigh, she taps the power button. The sun's rays beat down on the pavement and desert surrounding us. Cloudless skies and cracked sand seem to stretch into an endless abyss of nothingness. The quiet and a belly full of carbs make my eyelids grow heavy.

"Tell me about your kids, Delores." I hope conversation wards off my sleepiness.

She jumps at the sound of my voice. Did I wake her? With

her eyes hidden behind large dark sunglasses, I couldn't tell if she was sleeping.

"Sorry." I didn't mean to scare her.

She twists toward the back of the car and sticks her half bag of chips into one of the brown paper bags. When she shifts back around, she straightens her posture, smoothing her hands down the front of her blouse. She pulls down the passenger visor, checks her reflection, then rubs her fingers across the corners of her lips. She *was* asleep.

"You've not told me much about them. The only time you mentioned them was during our Silver Alert crisis," I say, curious.

Delores's face reddens. Her usual bright smile morphs into a grimace. "My kids." She crosses her arms across her chest. "Where do I begin?"

Worried I've brought up a sore subject, I focus on the road ahead again. I should tell her she doesn't need to talk about them if it brings up bad feelings, but a part of me wants to know why she's angry with them. What did they do? Do they ignore her like Emma ignores me? Or worse yet, keep secrets from her?

"I have three kids," she says, then names them with as much enthusiasm as someone reading a grocery list. "Harper is my oldest. She's fifty. Lucas is my middle child and only son. He's forty-eight. Camila is my youngest. She was an oops baby and turned forty last month. All three of them are as different as night and day, but all of them are annoying."

"Dave and I would have loved to have more kids," I say wistfully, ignoring Delores's sarcasm. "It just didn't work out for us."

"Oh, it's great—until they gang up on you," she snaps. "Since my husband passed, my kids have been trying to put me in assisted living." Heat radiates from her side of the car.

"Why?" I shake my head in disbelief.

"Last year, right after my husband passed, his cat, which I never liked, worked his way between my legs when I was outside checking the mail." Her angry tone turns bitter. "The cat and I got all tangled up, and I fell. I tried to catch myself before I hit the concrete curb at the end of the driveway and broke my wrist. My kids made the incident into a big deal, claiming I couldn't take care of myself anymore. They took the cat, which was fine by me, then they started treating me like I was fragile and incompetent." Her volume grows. "Who do they think took care of their father when he was dying of cancer? It sure wasn't them." She takes a deep breath in, then lowers her voice.

"Then there was the business. Hank and I ran a hardwood store. I wasn't ready to sell, but they kept badgering me with their incessant, illogical reasoning. Hank was the face of the store. He was knowledgeable about tools and building, but I ran the business side. I did all the ordering, payroll, bookkeeping, taxes, and more. You get the idea, I'm sure. But my kids never gave me any credit, believing their dad did it all. They always put him on a pedestal, and I didn't want to mar that image. They saw me as the ditz in eccentric clothing behind the counter. I loved Hank, so I went along with it."

She takes a sip of her soda. "Agnus and Bea also encouraged me to sell so I could be free from the responsibilities of owning a business. They had all retired. We could finally take the trips we never had time for when we were younger because of work and raising our families. So, I gave in and sold the store to a dear friend of Hank. I let my kids have their little *win*, but that wasn't enough. Like I said earlier, they want me to move to an assisted living arrangement or move in with one of them, heaven forbid." She rolls her eyes and pounds her fist on the dashboard. "Do I look like I need to go to a home to you, Sarah?"

I give an emphatic "No." I try to imagine Delores not living life on her terms. "Do your kids even know you?"

"Not really," she says sadly. "They haven't lived near home in years, and rarely visit."

"Have you ever tried talking to them?" I'm incredulous they think of her as a frail woman who needs someone to care for her. Delores is the strongest woman I know. I wish I was more like her.

"Talking to them is like beating my head against a brick wall. Harper and Camila ramrod everything, while Lucas stands by, afraid to contradict them."

"I'm sorry, Delores." Why do families have to be so hard? My thoughts turn to Emma. "Life seems to turn out a lot different than what you once pictured in your head. I feel disillusioned sometimes, like I've lived so cautiously, trying to do everything right, but the results still turned out wrong." I frown.

"Yes," says Delores. "My husband exercised, ate right, kept track of his cholesterol and blood pressure. He never smoked. He was the picture of health. Until he wasn't. He got a cancer diagnosis during a routine wellness visit and died six months later. I've learned that no matter how carefully you live your life or play by someone's made-up rules, things don't always turn out like you thought they would. Right now, I'm supposed to be living my golden years with my sweetheart, but I'm fighting with my children instead."

"With the weight of what you've told me, how are you so happy?" I'm hopeful she'll give me the formula to being happier in my own life.

"I'm not always happy, but I try to enjoy each day as it comes—thankful for another day. None of us are guaranteed tomorrow." Delores pauses, placing her hand on her chest. "I try to focus on my blessings instead of my problems. Some days, the silver lining is harder to find than on others, but there's always something to be grateful for *every day*," she says. "Do you want to know what I'm grateful for today?"

I nod my head.

"You, Sarah. I'm grateful for you."

Her words embrace my heart like a warm fuzzy blanket. "Thank you," I say, my voice filled with emotion. "Your kids are so lucky to have you."

Silence fills the car again. Before I can formulate the right words to confess how grateful I am for our new friendship or how I've secretly wished my mom would have been like her, Delores yelps. "I need to use a bathroom."

"Here?" I ask, jolted out of my thoughts.

"We just passed a public rest area sign. Didn't you see it?"

"No." I blink.

"It said it's the last one for sixty miles. We have to stop, Sarah. I drank all that soda."

"A rest stop?" I clench the steering wheel with my fingers. "I can't stop."

"What? Why?" She snaps her head in my direction.

"My grandma made me swear to never stop at one."

Delores scowls. "Why would she do that?"

A hot flush creeps across my cheeks. *She's going to think I'm crazy.* I wince before answering, "She said there could be perverts there."

Delores slaps her forehead with her palm. "You've gotta be kidding me."

I shake my head.

"What in the world was your grandma smoking? You're telling me you've never stopped at a rest area?" Delores's blue eyes bulge.

"Never." I shrug.

The rest stop appears on the right side of the highway. "I'll take my chances. Turn now," Delores commands.

Painted arrows point to the off-ramp. I jerk the steering wheel to the right without lowering our speed. Our bags of snacks topple over, spilling their contents all over the floor.

"Whoa." Delores holds onto the passenger grab handle.

"Oops. Sorry." My face heats. I brake, slowing the car enough to follow the side road leading to a long brick building. Once parked, Delores races to the designated women's bathroom. I exit the car and stretch my legs, keeping a watchful eye out for any suspicious travelers. "Perverts."

My cell chimes. Emma's picture flashes on the screen. Delores hasn't come out yet, so I answer the call, surveying my surroundings. "Hi, sweetie."

"Hi, Mom. Where are you? I've been trying to call you all day," Emma scolds.

"Hmm, I don't have any missed calls from you," I say. "My phone must be messing up again." Or there's no cell signal out here in the middle of nowhere. "Is everything okay?"

"Yes, Philip and I are fine. I was just wondering if you got the box of stuff I sent."

"What box?" My mouth falls open. I can't believe she thinks I'm at home. Hasn't she looked at the recent photos or texts I've sent her? Of course not. She's been ignoring them like usual. And what about Dave? Hasn't he told her I ran away? *They share everything.* I smirk. The pulse in my temple begins to pound.

"I sent you what was left in my dorm. We don't have room for all of it here. I thought you could store it in my bedroom until I can sort through it later," Emma says.

"I haven't checked. Maybe your dad has it." Shrugging in surrender, I glance up at the sky.

"Okaaay," Emma says, probably confused. "What's going on, Mom? You sound different."

Incredulous, I reply, "Nothing. I'm just in the middle of something."

Delores returns and gives me a thumbs-up, mouthing, "no perverts."

"It's Emma." I point to the phone.

Delores smiles but doesn't leave my side.

Emma pauses for a long time, then says, "Well, that's why I called. I guess I better go. Philip is waiting on me to go to dinner."

"Okay, then," I say.

Emma's end clicks. She doesn't say "goodbye" or "I love you." I'm left holding a silent phone to my ear.

"Did you tell her we're coming to visit after Las Vegas?" Delores's questioning eyes search mine.

I bite my lower lip. "I thought we could surprise her."

She nods, but a shadow of doubt crosses her face.

# CHAPTER THIRTY

My mind drifts with the rhythmic clicking of the wheels on the pavement and Delores's soft snores. Why didn't I tell Emma I might visit her?

Because I haven't decided if it's a good idea or not.

The closer we get to Phoenix, the heavier the weight sitting on my chest. I've pictured three different scenarios. All three begin with me knocking on her apartment door, anxiously waiting for her to open it.

Scenario One: Emma throws open the door and hugs me like she doesn't ever want to let go. She's happy to see me, and we live happily ever after. I smile. I like that scenario.

Scenario Two: Emma's not home. I don't see her at all. This one makes me a little sad, but also somewhat relieved. The idea of putting off disappointment, even though it doesn't resolve anything, is classic me.

Scenario Three: Emma opens the door with a scowl on her face. She lets me in, but it's obvious she's put out by my presence. She can't get rid of me fast enough. Each time this scenario pops into my brain, a lump forms in my throat. Not knowing the outcome in advance has my heart tied in knots.

In the distance, a large blue-and-white sign looms on the side of the road. I squint, trying to read the words. No luck. It's too far away. I hope it's not a detour. I've been on enough of those lately. I turn off the cruise control, and our rental slows down. The closer we get, the clearer the words become. Certain I'm seeing a mirage, I rub my eyes. That doesn't help. The sign remains, confirming it's not my imagination. It reads: The Loneliest Road in America.

I pull the car onto the shoulder and glance at Delores. She's sleeping soundly. I leave the car running, quietly open my door, and step onto the pavement. The hum of the car engine is the only sound. No birds chirp, no wind blows, no sign of life—only desolate silence.

I walk to the sign, then, for some unknown reason, extend my right hand and trace the word "Loneliest". Sweat trickles down my temples from the sun beating against my back, but weirdly, the metal under my fingertips is cold. An intense longing strikes me in the chest, knocking the air out of me.

A whiff of Delores's perfume snaps me out of my trance. I hadn't heard her climb out of the car or come up next to me.

"So, why are we stopped in the middle of the desert again?" she asks, worry lines across her forehead.

"No breakdown this time," I assure her. "Just thinking."

She glances at me. "About what?"

I lock eyes with her, pausing to gather the right words. "I was wondering about the person who named this The Loneliest Highway. Did that person stand in this solitary desert, and the loneliness of this place overpowered him in that moment, or was it a lingering sense that never left him—no matter his surroundings or circumstances?"

Delores remains quiet, listening. Her presence comforts

me. Her light-blue eyes never stray from me. No judgment crosses her face.

"There's a difference between being alone and feeling alone, isn't there." It's more a statement than a question.

"Yes." Her eyes soften. "You can feel alone on a crowded city street, in a room full of people, and even amongst your friends and family."

"I know," I say. "It's weird, isn't it?"

"Yes, it is. Even though I have friends and family who love me, when Hank passed away, I felt alone. I had a hard time adjusting. Grief-stricken, I viewed the world through loss. The invitations to join my friends became less frequent. The girls had just about given up on me. But after a year of sitting in an empty house, I decided my time on earth was short. I didn't want to waste another day wallowing in self-pity. While I was still grieving, I realized I needed my friends. I reached out to them. I planned adventures and tried new things. And let me tell you, Sarah, it was the best decision I ever made. Now I get to spend time with the people I love—like Agnus, Bea, Irene ... and you."

Grateful to be included in the list of women I admire, warmth floods my heart again.

"I still have bad days. We all do. And I still miss my Hank every day." Delores dabs the moisture at the corners of her eyes. "But each morning, I wake up and decide to make it a good day," she says, smiling.

"I'm starting to realize I've chosen to feel alone. I've kept people at arm's length to protect my heart," I admit.

"But it comes at a terrible price," Delores says.

I nod, knowing she's right. "Can I ask you another question?"

She wipes sweat from her forehead with the back of her hand. "Sure, what's your question?"

"Are you clairvoyant?" I narrow my eyes.

Loud laughter blasts from her small frame.

"What?" I raise my hands defensively. Heat rises into my neck, making me hotter, if that's possible. "You always seem to know what I'm thinking. It's a valid question."

The mischievous glint disappears from her eyes. Her red lips press into a tight line. "Yes, just call me Madam Delores." Straight-faced, she uses a horrible Romanian accent.

I groan. She snickers, the playful light returning to her eyes. "My mother always said I was good at reading people. I'm perceptive. And you, my dear, are an easy read. You wear your emotions on your face. Hasn't anyone told you that before?"

"No." Is that why I rarely win an argument with Dave or Emma? Does my expression show I'm wavering?

"I guess I better not say what you're thinking now," Delores teases. I give her a squinty stare. She chuckles. "Now it's my turn to ask you a question." I wait for her to needle me about something personal, but she asks, "Have you ever watched any of those desert movies where the mutant people try to kill the lost tourists?"

"Ha ha, always the jokester," I state in a sarcastic tone.

"No, I'm serious." She clutches her hand to her chest, and her eyes widen. "Dead serious." She lowers her voice an octave, and her lips turn down in a grimace instead of the mischievous smirk I've grown accustomed to.

A flash of light flickers in the distance behind her. The hairs on my arms rise. Squinting to see if it happens again, I'm reminded of the quietness here. No wind, no wildlife, not even a bird flying in the air. The sun casts long shadows across the desert floor. Even the sparse plant life seems foreboding. Another light flashes several feet from the first one. Could someone or something be watching us? Are they using code to communicate? Adrenaline pulses through my veins, shooting straight to my extremities. I take off like a rocket, yelling, "Run, before the mutant people get us!"

Behind me, I hear the clang and jingle of Delores's bracelets smashing into one another, along with the quick click of her clunky heels hitting the asphalt. She might as well be wearing a dinner bell. Remembering she's older than me, I pivot, run back to her, and loop my arm through hers. We scurry to the car as fast as our legs will carry us, throw open our doors, jump into our seats, and click the doors locked.

"Time to go," Delores exclaims.

The tires squeal as I peel onto the highway. Pushing the accelerator to the floor, I'm relieved to watch the barren scenery fly by. In our hurry to leave, I didn't check the map on my phone. I'm not sure when we're supposed to exit.

"Can you check the directions?" I point to my cell lying on the dash.

She grabs it, checks the map, then bursts out in a fit of giggles. "You're not going to believe this."

I search her face. "What? Tell me why you've suddenly lost your senses."

She covers her mouth, stifling a laugh that ends in a snort. With wide eyes and a smirk, she says, "The next road we take to Las Vegas is called 'Extraterrestrial Highway.'"

# CHAPTER THIRTY-ONE

After driving for a while, we forget about the possibility of extraterrestrials in flying saucers taking us to their mother ship. Added lanes and heavier traffic indicate Vegas is close. The sun skims the earth's surface, creating layers of orange, purple, and yellow on the horizon. Millions of brilliant lights twinkle as we draw closer to the strip. The Welcome to Fabulous Las Vegas sign is posted ahead.

Delores can't contain her excitement. She oohs and aahs, squirming in her seat as we pass Mandalay Bay, Luxor, and Excaliber.

"Where to, Delores? Today's your day." I glance at her and grin.

"Caesar's Palace." She beams.

"Caesar's Palace it is." I laugh. "Let's see if they have any rooms available. My treat."

She doesn't argue. Instead, she leans forward, perching on the edge of her seat. Her eyes are wide as she takes in the bright lights of the Vegas Strip. My heart flutters at her glowing face. Flashes of an excited Emma play as I recall the time we took her to Disney World.

We park but, eager to mill around the main floor, we leave our bags in the car. After I pay for our one-night stay, we plan to come back for our luggage later. Once we enter the casino, we're met with the flashing lights of gaming machines and a haze of cigarette smoke. Bells ring and people cheer each time a winner is declared at one of the gaming tables. The chink of coins hitting metal, followed by a whirring buzz, echoes throughout the casino each time someone pulls a slot machine. My temples begin to pound from the noise, smoke, and bright lights, but I don't want to dampen Delores's celebration, so I smile at her. She's like a kid in a candy shop, roaming from one game to the next.

Finally, she stops at a table with a red-and-black spinning circle. A ball bounces from one number to another. The man controlling the wheel yells out the winning number when the ball lands in place.

"I've always wanted to play the red-and-black spinny thing," Delores says. "You know, pretend I'm a high roller." She winks at me.

"You mean the roulette wheel?" A young lady balancing a tray of drinks pauses next to us, and Delores nods. "You'll need to buy some chips."

"How much for a chip?" Delores asks the man controlling the wheel. He darts a glance at her, his bald head shining under the florescent lights. He's dressed impeccably in a black vest and matching slacks. His crisp white shirt is buttoned to the top. He wears a black bow tie and freshly shined black shoes.

"Five dollars," he says, then focuses on the gaming table.

Delores pulls her wallet out of her purse, retrieves a five-dollar bill, and hands him the money. He points his finger to the table. A shadow of confusion passes across Delores's face before she nods and places the money on the green felt. With one quick sweep of his arm across the table, her bill, along with the money three men and one other woman laid down, disappears into a locked box. The dealer slides stacks of chips to the other participants. He gives Delores a single chip. She clutches it in the palm of her hand. The others place their chips on various number and color combinations.

The dealer stares at Delores, drumming his fingers on the wooden frame. The other participants grow restless. One finishes his drink and slams his glass on the table. Another man checks his watch. The woman taps her foot. Four sets of eyes bore down on Delores.

"Ma'am, if you're playing this round, you need to place your bet," the dealer states.

She nods, then lets out a loud sigh. She slides her chip to rest on red twenty-three, then crosses her fingers.

The roulette man spins the wheel.

"Come on, Snake Eyes," Delores yells.

"Wrong game, ma'am," he says over the clacking of the spinning wheel. The ball bounces from one number to the next, jockeying for a spot to rest.

After a few moments, the wheel loses momentum. The clacking slows. The ball falls into one of the canoes.

The roulette dealer calls black eleven. With another sweep of his right arm, all the chips disappear. No winners this time. Delores looks like someone slapped her.

"Maybe you should stick to slot machines," the roulette man suggests.

She gives a loud humph, then adds, "Why would I do that? I don't gamble."

The roulette man narrows his eyes, and his bushy eyebrows bunch together.

"She's joking," I groan, then release an awkward titter.

He shakes his head, then returns his focus to the table.

We gather our purses, but before we leave, Delores asks, "Which way to the gift shop?"

The roulette man points to the other side of the casino.

On our way, Delores asks, "Did I ever tell you that the girls and I play cards once a week?"

I shake my head.

"Rummy, Uno, Hearts, those kinds of games. We play every Tuesday afternoon. The girls wanted me to invite you. They said they won't take no for an answer. Well, unless you have other obligations, I suppose." She winks.

I've never had close friends as an adult. My only interactions with other women have been working with other parents through Emma's school functions or the soccer team boosters. I never made any friends through those groups, only casual acquaintances. The coordinators for those functions usually gave me the obligatory "Thanks for helping out," then sent me on my way. Although now that I think about it, how hard did I try to make friends? Somewhere deep down, I decided it was one thing to be rejected for the face I presented to the world but devastating to be rejected for showing them my real self. So I slapped on a smile, did what was required, and enjoyed being a part of Emma's school life without giving too much of myself away.

The fact Delores knows the real me and still wants to be my friend astounds me.

"I look forward to it." I'm humbled by the invitation.

She stops. "Well, isn't this something."

My eyes dart from her face to the huge ivory archway above us and the large pillars topped with Roman sculptures ahead.

"This is way more than the small souvenir shop I was expecting." I'm awed by the painted domed ceiling and marble tile floors. We stroll through the archway. The ceiling becomes an azure sky with large, puffy white clouds. The sky seems to move with us as we wander the forum.

Numerous high-end stores line both sides of the hallway. They're out of my price range, but I'm not here to shop. I'm fascinated by the large fountain surrounded by Roman statues. My eyes land on a particular Roman goddess nearest to us. I squint, focused on her face.

"Hello." Delores nudges me. "Earth to Sarah."

"Oh, sorry." I shake my head. "I can't quit looking at her."

"Who?" Delores lifts an eyebrow.

"Her," I whisper, leaning closer to Delores then pointing to the statue. "She moved."

"You're hallucinating again, aren't you?" she chuckles.

"No. And I wasn't hallucinating at the diner, either, if you remember," I huff.

Shrugging, she veers in the direction I pointed. She crosses her arms over her chest. Arching an eyebrow, she studies the statue. When nothing happens, she gives an exacerbated sigh. Then ... the statue blinks. Delores jumps, clutching her hand to her chest.

"See, I told you. Now who's hallucinating?" I smirk.

Her cheeks turn pink, but she raises her chin. "Oh, I've heard of people dressing up, imitating the statues. I just never thought they would look so legit." She smooths her hands down her blue silk blouse.

"Mm-hmm, sure," I mumble.

Delores pretends to ignore my gloating and points to a little shop tucked between two larger stores. "While you were staring at that statue," she says in a sarcastic tone, "I asked where we could find charms for our bracelets. The nice man I talked to said the store over there might have some."

Before I can comment, Delores pivots and makes a beeline

toward the store, disappearing inside. Worn out from the day's events, I trail behind. Her unlimited energy boggles me. The woman must have twenty years on me, but she runs circles around me.

I haven't even made it through the doorway when I hear her.

"Sarah, look what I found!" Something shiny hangs from a square of white cardboard between her fingers. "Handcuffs and fuzzy dice." Loud cackles blast through the store, catching the attention of the other customers. For once, my face doesn't flush.

When I reach her, she holds up the tiny silver handcuff charm once again. Then she hands me the other charm she laid on the counter—a small pair of fuzzy red dice.

"I've got it this time. We'll need two of each." I hand my credit card to the cashier. "Dave's going to have a lot of questions when he sees my new bracelet." I wince. I can't even imagine how that conversation will play out. What will he think of me after all my adventures? I push those thoughts away to deal with later.

Once our purchase is complete, we leave the store in search of a place to sit. Conveniently, there's a bench outside the gift shop. After removing the charms from the plastic bag, Delores and I attach them to our bracelets.

"What a time we've had." She clasps her bracelet back on her wrist.

"We sure have. The best." Warmth fills my chest. With a grateful smile, I say, "We'll definitely have some stories to share when we get home. And to think it all began when I sat down at a table of strangers and ate pie."

Delores chuckles. Her charm bracelet jingles when she pats my hand.

We face the fountain, not saying more. A few people are

walking around the forum. My shoulders relax as I listen to the rush of water streaming down over the rocks at the basin of the fountain. A large statue of Poseidon watches over his domain while Pegasus and other Roman statues guard the pool. I close my eyes, inhaling and exhaling deep breaths. This is the most relaxed I've felt in days. I relish the weightlessness of this moment.

"Mother?" A woman's shrill voice interrupts my peace.

Eyes wide open, I jerk my head toward the voice. I don't know the woman, but she stares pointedly in our direction. She rushes toward us with another woman and a man on her heels. Warning bells blare in my head, and dread has my stomach churning. Good grief, now what?

# CHAPTER THIRTY-TWO

Scowling and red-faced, Delores jumps to her feet. Once the threesome reaches us, she demands, "How did you know I was here?" Her eyes narrow while she waits for an answer.

The striking woman with coiffed blonde hair leads the charge. She wears an impeccable navy suit with a Louis Vuitton purse hanging over her shoulder. She glances down her nose at me with haughty regard. Her dark-blue glare pins me to my seat.

I rise and stand next to Delores, unsure who these people are or what they want.

The blonde's tall, erect posture looms over us. Can we take her?

But then the shorter woman moves close to Delores and gives her a big hug. "Hi, Mom."

My muscles relax as the threat of danger subsides, but Delores remains rigid even after returning her daughter's hug. "Sarah, these are my kids," she says with a tight smile. "This is my youngest daughter, Camila." She gives the young woman who hugged her a side squeeze.

We exchange smiles. Camila's petite like her mom but doesn't have Delores's black hair or light-blue eyes. She does wear her hair in a short blonde bob, similar to Delores's style. I see the resemblance between her and her older sister, but Camila's not intimidating. Instead, she has a warmth and friendliness about her, much like her mother.

Delores points to her son next. He stands awkwardly beside his big sister, his hands shoved into the pockets of his black dress pants. He glances from one area of the forum to another, never making eye contact with either Delores or me.

"This is Lucas." She draws his attention. His eyes dart to mine. He gives me a curt nod, then blinks at Delores. Except for his taller height, he's a male replica of Delores. He's around six feet tall, with the same ebony hair and pale-blue eyes. He might be considered handsome, but his nervous tics distract from his good looks. Anxiety rises in my chest.

"And last but not least, my oldest daughter, Harper."

I smile at her. She frowns while tapping her Gucci black leather pump.

Leaning toward me, Delores says, "If I were to guess, Harper dragged Lucas here against his will. He can't say no to her. And Camila never wants to be left out, so she tagged along." She shifts her focus back to her children. "Am I right?"

"I'm only going to ask you one more time. Why are you here, and how did you find me?" All three adults seem to wilt before Delores as she speaks in an authoritative voice.

Shrinking under the weight of her piercing stare, Camila blurts, "We've been so worried about you, Mom. When we found out you didn't come back with the tour bus, we feared someone had kidnapped you or you were hurt somewhere with no one to help you."

"I'm not as fragile as you children seem to think," Delores huffs. "Do you know how much trouble you put us through with your silly Silver Alert?"

Lucas diverts his gaze to the marble floor. Camila peeks over at Harper, who has quit tapping her shoe.

"That doesn't answer the second question. How did you know where to find me?"

"Harper put a tracker on your cell phone," Camila says.

"Thanks a lot, you tattletale," Harper snaps.

Camila blushes, then shuffles her feet to stand by Lucas.

"A what?" Delores shrieks so loud a group of tourists walking by stops and stares at us.

Lucas's eyes dart their direction. He offers them an apologetic smile, then ducks his head, visibly shrinking beside Camila. "Can we take this somewhere else?" he asks in a low, pleading voice.

"We have a hotel room here." I hope my offer will move us away from the gawking onlookers. Lucas gives me an appreciative nod. "Delores, you can take your kids to our room. I'll hang out down here and give you all some privacy."

My fingers tremble as I pull the room key from my purse and pass it to Delores.

"Oh, no, you don't." She brushes my hand away. "You're coming too."

Wide-eyed with disbelief, I argue, "Delores, this is a family matter." I push the key toward her closed fist.

"I didn't leave you when the police officer took you to jail." She grabs my arm.

My face flames from embarrassment, even making my ears and the roots of my hair burn. The shoppers leave a wide berth around us as they shoot suspicious glances our way. I scan the forum, searching for a quick exit, but Delores's and her kids' raised voices escalate—drawing the attention of a mall security cop. His eyes lock on mine. He crooks his head toward his right shoulder to talk into a small two-way radio, focusing on me the whole time. He leans forward. The Segway heads straight for us.

"I'll go! I'll go," I shout over Delores and her kids and pull on her arm.

Before I can usher her to the nearby elevator, a deep male voice asks, "Is everything okay here?" Intensified by the bright florescent ceiling lights, his badge flashes the word "Security."

Delores and her kids stop mid-argument and swing around to face the large man on the Segway.

Surprisingly, Harper's rigid posture relaxes. Her lips part and curve upward, displaying perfect white teeth. Her smile transforms her face. She looks so different than the angry woman I've seen up until now.

"Everything's fine, Officer," she says in a honeyed tone. I furrow my eyebrows and tilt my head. Is she talking with a southern accent? "We're just catching up with my mom and her friend ..."

"Sarah," I fill in before the officer figures out Harper doesn't know me.

"It looked like you were arguing and causing a public disturbance." His eyes flick from Delores to each of her kids, then narrow on me.

I gulp.

"It's been a long day, Officer. We're tired and ready to find our rooms," Harper explains.

The mall cop shifts his focus back on her.

"We won't cause any more disturbances. I promise." She flashes him an icky saccharine smile, then glances at Lucas and Camila. They both nod. "Could you point us in the direction of the nearest elevator, please?" She places French-tipped manicured fingers on his arm. "And we'll be on our way." She winks.

He doesn't smile but pauses.

Is he trying to decide whether to let us go or not? My stomach tenses.

His radio crackles and sputters to life. A voice on the other end of the radio speaks, but I can't quite make out the words—something about a possible shoplifter? Whatever the issue, it takes precedence over our public disturbance. Without saying anything more to us, the mall cop points to an elevator down the hallway, tips his hat, and glides down the corridor until he's out of view.

I exhale a long breath, then escort Delores and her family to the elevator before they start arguing again. We ride to the third floor. Our suite, 312, is only a few steps away, the first door to the left of the elevator.

Once inside our room, Delores swings her arms out and spins in a circle. "Oh my, Sarah. I can't wait to tell the girls about our swanky accommodations." Her dancing eyes flit from one area of the spacious living room to another.

I wanted to surprise her with a luxury suite. I got a good deal since the hotel wasn't full tonight, and separate bedrooms were a bonus. I was so excited when I booked the suite, but with the arrival of her kids, I'm not sure we'll get to enjoy it.

"Can you afford this, Mom?" Harper snipes, breaking the spell.

Delores stops mid-step. Her beaming smile droops. "Yes, I can. But I didn't have to." She smiles at me. "Sarah insisted on paying for it since today's my birthday."

Camila gasps. Harper's eyes widen. Lucas gulps, then lowers his gaze to the floor.

"Oh, Mom." Camila's voice breaks. She slaps her palm to her forehead. "How could we have forgotten?"

"Probably because you were too busy creating havoc." Delores scowls at her grown children. "Do you know that Sarah had to wear handcuffs because of the Silver Alert you all concocted? And what's this about a tracker on my phone? Why would you do such a thing?"

I feel out of place here, but Delores is my friend. On one hand, I hate leaving her to fight this battle alone. But on the other hand, I wish the plush wall-to-wall carpet would swallow me up.

Harper steps forward. Delores stands her ground, hands on her hips, a force to be reckoned with—all five feet of her. The other two siblings look relieved to be out of the hot seat, shielded behind their sister.

"Do you remember when you fell and broke your wrist, Mom?" Harper clears her throat. "Of course you do. Well, anyway, when you went to the doctor's office to have your wrist reset and a cast put on it, I stayed in the waiting area. You left your purse with me. Remember?" She doesn't wait for a response. "While you were gone, I took your phone out of your bag and downloaded the tracking app, connecting our phones."

Delores nods. Her face is expressionless when she says, "I see."

"I did it out of concern." Harper explains her actions as if talking to a child.

An invisible electric charge fires between mother and daughter. I don't know if they feel it, but the words "danger, danger" blare in my brain.

Delores makes a thoughtful pose before saying smugly, "Tracking my whereabouts seems like a violation of my privacy. I wonder what my lawyer would say about this?"

Harper's lips press into a thin grim line.

"It's for your own good," Lucas chimes in. A flash of regret crosses his face. He winces and lowers his eyes to the floor, retreating into the background again.

"It is, is it?" Delores challenges. "Then I want trackers on your phones too. Half the time I call, you don't pick up. Should I be worried? You might be lying in a ditch somewhere. Isn't that what us moms usually think?" She releases an acrid laugh. "And wouldn't it be fun for me to pop up during your vacation? Maybe cause a little chaos while I'm there?"

Harper's eyes widen, and worry lines try to form across her Botox-smooth forehead. "I hardly think that's necessary." She stomps her foot.

"Like someone once said, 'Turnabout is fair play,'" Delores replies.

Harper and Delores stare each other down, neither willing to give an inch.

After several minutes of awkward silence, Delores says, "One day, the time may come when I need someone to keep tabs on me, but until then, we all have trackers on our phones, or none of us do." She folds her arms across her chest. "Your choice."

Harper peers over her shoulder at her siblings. They both shrug. With a loud huff, Harper throws her palm out.

Delores walks over to the couch, pulls her cell out of her bag, then hands it to her daughter. She keeps a watchful eye on Harper and the cell.

With her manicured index finger, Harper holds the GPS app down until it shakes, then clicks delete. "Satisfied?" she says in a biting tone.

"Very." Delores takes her phone back and tucks it into her pants pocket. "Now that I know how you've found me, my next question is, why? And don't you dare say you thought I was lost. One phone call would have dismissed that concern." She rolls her eyes.

Harper nods at her sister, who has been quiet until now.

Pulling a document out of her oversized purple bag, Camila steps toward her mom. "We brought Power of Attorney papers for you to sign." She grimaces. "Harper had them drawn up, but we need to know who you select as your power of attorney." A flush creeps across her cheeks as she shoves the papers at Delores.

Delores takes them but doesn't even glance at them. "Wow, you've been busy little bees," she says in a wry tone.

*I should not be here. I should not be here.* The phrase plays on a continuous loop in my brain. With light steps, I slowly back away, hoping to disappear unnoticed and hide away in a nearby bedroom. I've only taken a few steps when the floor below me creaks.

Delores whirls, her eyes pinning me in place. Frozen, I watch as she turns back to her kids. "Since you are all in a big fat hurry for me to pick someone to control me, I choose Sarah."

The room explodes with yelling. Delores's kids shoot daggers at me with their eyes while trying to reason with their mom.

The blood drains from my face. My knees wobble.

"Mom, be serious," Camila pleads.

Harper throws her arms in the air. "You're being ridiculous." Her lips pucker like she's sucked on a lemon.

Lucas gives an exasperated "Whatever," then drops onto the couch behind him. He's done.

I'm done. This is all too much.

While Delores and her girls continue arguing, I escape into the nearest bedroom. Plopping down on the bed, I grab the remote from the end table and turn on the TV, raising the volume loud enough to drown out their conversation.

After zoning out on an old black-and-white Western for an hour, I hear a quiet rap on the door.

"Sarah?" Delores questions from the other side.

I pad to the door and pull it open.

"Can I come in?" Her voice cracks.

I nod, but not before peering past Delores. Her kids are still here, all sitting on the couch, shoulders hunched as they stare at their phones.

Delores enters my room and closes the door. With tears in her eyes, she says softly, "I'm so sorry. I never meant for you to get caught up in all this drama. I know they haven't made a good first impression, but they really are great kids. They're just misguided sometimes." Her lips form a sad smile. "I love them with all my heart, but I've let them get away with too much, especially since their father passed. We usually don't argue—that much." She winces. "I just go along with whatever they want. Having you here gave me the courage to stand up for myself."

Me? My mouth falls open, but I have no response. Delores doesn't seem afraid of anything. Her gutsy spirit and can-do attitude are what I admire most about her.

"Anyway, thank you for the wonderful birthday surprise. I hate that I won't get to enjoy it, but it's enough knowing you did it for me."

"You're leaving?" Heaviness fills my heart.

"I'm going to fly home with my kids. They're booking us flights home tonight." She frowns. Her eyes are lackluster.

"Are you sure you have to go? Is this really what you want?" I study her expression for an answer. Is this her idea, or have her kids worn her down?

Delores nods, then with a loud sigh, replies, "While their methods were wrong, they do have a point. I need to get my affairs in order. I've put it off because it's not fun to think about. They're going to come with me to my doctor and lawyer to check off all the boxes, if you know what I mean." Her body seems to wilt when she mutters, "Getting old stinks."

"If you're what old looks like, then sign me up." I chuckle, then give her a heartfelt hug. "You might be my best friend," I whisper before I release her.

Delores laughs. Tears glisten in both of our eyes now.

"You were kidding when you said you were making me your power of attorney, right?" I titter but wait anxiously for her to confirm.

She shrugs, giving me one of her mischievous grins again. I wish I knew when she was serious. I shake my head.

"I guess I better go see if my kids are ready to head to the airport." She sighs again.

My chest tightens with realization. If she leaves tonight, I'll be here alone. "Maybe I should fly home too." I pray she'll agree.

She takes my hands in hers, locks eyes with me, then says, "Since I didn't get to fully enjoy my present, I have a birthday wish."

"Oh?" I hesitate—a little wary of what she will ask.

"I want you to enjoy your night here. Order room service. Go to the spa. Then bright and early tomorrow, go see that beautiful girl of yours. Work things out with her before you end up in a mess like mine. Can you do that for me, Sarah?"

My hands grow clammy. An overwhelming sense of dread envelops me as I think about making the rest of the trip alone. Even when I refused to get on the tour bus days ago, claiming I'd strike out on my own, Delores saved me.

As if reading my mind again, Delores says, "You're stronger than you think, Sarah." She squeezes my hands. "Do it for Emma. Do it for *you*."

# CHAPTER THIRTY-THREE

W hen I leave Las Vegas, it isn't long before I'm driving down the deserted highway again. I'm lonely without Delores's company. The quiet has me drowning in my thoughts. The closer I get to Phoenix, the more the knots in my stomach clench. Will Emma be happy to see me?

Every instinct tells me to turn the car around, head back to Vegas, and fly home. But the cruise control is set, and the car practically drives itself on the straight roads, racing closer to Emma's new home.

*Don't be ridiculous*, I tell myself over and over. But doubt and panic won't stop fighting with my reason. Adrenaline pumps through my veins, making my head hurt. I can't do this, I decide. With a disappointed sigh, I scan for a side road, overpass, or anywhere I can turn around.

Up ahead, a green road sign stands on the side of the highway. As I cruise closer, no restaurants, gas stations, or motels are listed on the sign—only an arrow pointing to a turnoff. Rotating the steering wheel to the right, I follow the arrows. As the SUV climbs the ramp, an old church appears at the top of the hill. Even though the white siding is in dire need of a fresh coat of paint, the stained-glass windows and bell tower add a rustic beauty to the small church. Rays of sunshine through the nebulous clouds beam down on its roof. No vehicles sit in the dirt lot. Only scrubby patches of grass and sand surround the building. I park in front of the white wooden door, climb out of the car, and walk around the church.

The hot wind whips my hair away from my face. A tumbleweed blows under a wooden hitching post, and a dirt devil whirls in the distance.

Dave would be so upset with me if he knew I had stopped to check out an abandoned church on a deserted highway. But the warm sun on my face, the wind rustling through scrubby patches of grass, and a high-pitched coo of a nearby dove calm my frayed nerves. With something new to focus on, my brain quiets, allowing me to take deep breaths until my racing pulse slows.

I return to the front of the church. A small wooden sign hangs above the door: "Little Chapel on a Hill est. 1882." I reach out and twist the copper doorknob. Surprisingly, it's unlocked. The door creaks when I open it.

The church looks empty, but I peek inside before treading onto the old hardwood floors. Light floods the interior through four multicolored stained-glass windows—two on each side of the building. A large picture window at the front frames the view of the desert below. Six rows of solid oak pews stand on each side of the room, leaving an aisle in the middle. The scrolled arms at the end of each pew look hand-carved. I'm awed by the craftsmanship. I close my eyes, imaging nineteenth-century families arriving on horseback and in wagons, dressed in their best clothes.

The church I attended with my grandma and dad when I was a girl was small too. Memory reels play. Listening to the preacher's sermon while chewing gum from Grandma's purse. The small congregation singing hymns like "Turn Your Eyes Upon Jesus" and "Amazing Grace."

I pick up an old hymnal from the pew across from me, carefully turning the worn yellow pages. Some fall to the floor after coming loose from the binding. I pick them up and tuck them back into the hymnal in front of a page with the corner folded over. My breath catches when I read the faded title. "Farther Along" by W.B. Stevens is printed at the top of the folded page. It was my dad's favorite hymn. An invisible blanket of peace envelops me.

Still holding the faded burgundy songbook, I sing. My voice starts off raspy from not using it in the quiet car but grows stronger as my vocal cords warm up. The words resurface from deep in my memory. I don't need the hymnal anymore, so I gaze at the rafters as I sing. "Farther along we'll know all about it, Farther along we'll understand why; Cheer up, my brother, live in the sunshine, We'll understand it all by and by."

I begin the second verse, but my voice cracks with emotion. There are so many things I wish I understood. Why did my mother abandon me? Why wasn't I enough to make her want to stay? I clench my hands. I could never do that to Emma. A daughter needs her mom.

My throat aches. And a mother needs her daughter. I can't understand the distance between us. What did I do wrong?

Laying the hymnal on the pew, I move to the beautiful hand-carved pulpit at the front. My fingers trace the palm marks imprinted on the sides of the pulpit where pastors held on while preaching the gospel.

Beside the pulpit sits a small cedar prayer bench. After laying my car keys and purse on the floor, I kneel. A kaleidoscope of colors from the stained-glass stream around me. Clasping my hands together in front of my face, I shut my eyes like I was taught in Sunday School so many years ago.

"Lord," I whisper and open my eyes as an unwanted tear trickles down my cheek and hits the hardwood, leaving a dark spot on the beautiful floor. "I need guidance. I need help. Will you help me?" My chin quivers.

The weight of a hand on my shoulder startles me. I jerk my head toward an elderly man kneeling beside me. With his eyes closed, he prays out loud—for me. I stare at him, frozen. He continues for several minutes, finishing with "Amen," then opens his eyes and turns to me.

My heart pounds. "Who are you?" Alarmed I'm not alone, the words rush out.

He lifts his lips into a closed-mouth smile, and his warm brown eyes crinkle at the corners. He doesn't seem threatening. In fact, he feels safe.

"I didn't mean to startle you," he says in a soft baritone and removes his hand from my shoulder. "I'm the caretaker of this property. I saw the car outside and wanted to make sure its owner was okay."

He pats my back and stands.

I grab my purse and keys, then push off the floor.

He's only a few steps from me when he extends his hand. "Hello. My name is William." He wears a yellow cardigan over a multicolored button-down checkered shirt and a brown pair of slacks, reminding me of my favorite TV personality—Mr. Rogers.

I shake his hand. "I'm Sarah."

William releases my hand, then takes a seat on the front pew. He pats the spot beside him.

My mind should be warning of stranger danger, but I feel

like I know him, even though my memory can't recall how. My feet carry me to the pew, seeming to have a mind of their own. I sit next to him.

William crosses one leg over the other, then folds his hands on his lap. "Well, Sarah, how did you get here?" he asks in a voice as comforting as one of my grandma's old quilts.

His question is loaded. "Here" could mean so many things. Without giving away any private details, I reply, "Honestly, I'm not sure. I was looking for a turnaround on the highway but ended up here instead."

"Why did you want to turn around?" His posture remains relaxed, but his eyes are an intense golden brown. They probe deep into mine.

"I couldn't decide whether to keep moving forward or go back," I confess.

"Hmm." He rubs his chin. He breaks eye contact and gazes through the picture window at the front of the church. "Go on."

Why I'm sitting here talking to a stranger baffles me. "I don't know. It's hard to explain." I look down at my hands. "For the past few years, I've been a little lost. On a whim, I ended up on an unplanned and unexpected journey. I've experienced a lot of things—some good, some bad." I chuckle, thinking of some of my adventures. "But now I'm on the last leg of my trip. I'm still not sure how to reconcile my past so it doesn't affect my future, how to navigate a good relationship with my daughter now that she's an adult, and how to find purpose at this time in my life when up until now she's been my purpose. The closer I get to my destination, the more my insides churn. I couldn't handle the doubt and anxiety anymore, so I decided to turn around. That's when I saw your church."

"Ah," he says. "What's ahead that's weighing on you?" His gaze shifts back to me.

"I have an uncomfortable conversation coming up. I'm not sure how it will turn out." I grimace. My heart is heavy from the weight of it all.

"How do you want it to go?" His eyes soften as he waits for my response.

I want Emma to see *me*—to try to understand our relationship from my point of view. I'm her biggest fan, but I need connection—phone calls, visits, to be included—in some small way—in her new life. And to ultimately know I've been a good mother—not perfect, but always there for her, helping her understand she's loved and valued. The heat in the little church seems to have increased several degrees under his scrutiny. Ready to leave before giving any more of myself away to this stranger, I rise. "It was nice meeting you, William, but I've taken enough of your time." I grab my purse and keys from the floor. Mentally, I'm sprinting to my car as fast as my feet will carry me, but my charm bracelet catches on the handle of my purse. I try to break my wrist free, but the clasp on the bracelet opens and charms scatter across the floor.

"Here, let me help you." William picks up the charms that landed farthest away. He brings them over, but before handing them to me asks, "Do you mind?"

I nod and give him the charms I picked up. I watch as he turns them over in his palm. "I bet there's a story behind each one." He smiles. His eyes search mine, the intensity replaced with a subtle golden-honey glow.

My face flames when he puts the handcuff charm in my palm, but I don't look at him. Instead, I attach the charm to my bracelet. One by one, he hands me Dorothy's red slippers, a cancan girl, fuzzy dice, a howling coyote, a picture of the Grand Canyon in a small oval bubble, and a miniature of the Kissing

Camels from Garden of the Gods. The last charm he deposits in my palm is a silver slice of pie.

Once I've attached all of them, I lay the bracelet across my wrist. William snaps the clasp shut. We exchange smiles.

I stare at the gaudy charm-filled band on my wrist, and a surge of gratitude fills my heart. Images of Agnus, Bea, and Delores flash before me. I'm reminded of their kindness—including me at their circular booth at the diner and rallying around me in the small aisle on the bus. I'm reminded of their humor—dancing arm in arm with each other on a stage in Kansas and catapulting our bodies into a monster truck.

Then my thoughts center on Delores. Tears spring to my eyes. She stood by me through my disappointing family search. Her humorous nature made being arrested somewhat bearable.

Even though the "girls" aren't here, their support and encouragement surround me. I can continue on to Phoenix, knowing I'm not truly alone.

Returning to the present, I remember I'm not alone in this church, either. I look up, ready to thank William for his kindness, but he's no longer standing by me. I scan the small sanctuary, calling out, "William?"

He doesn't respond.

I call out a few more times, but only an echo of my voice answers. Chill bumps rise on my forearms with the realization that there are no side exits in the church. There's only one way in and one way out. I hurry to the car. My rental is the only vehicle in the parking lot. No houses or buildings or any signs of civilization are anywhere near. It's only me. I remember my grandma reading me a verse one time—something about showing hospitality to strangers because you might be entertaining angels without knowing it.

My skin prickles. A rush of adrenaline has me racing to the car. My cell dings right after I lock the SUV doors.

Delores texted to let me know she made it home. A strong impulse to call her and share what happened battles against the desire to keep it to myself. With a long sigh, I decide some things are meant only for me.

# CHAPTER THIRTY-FOUR

The address on my phone matches the numbers posted on this apartment complex. I sigh, then park the car. My heart races. When I place my palm on my neck, the large vein pulses against my hand. I take a deep breath in and count—one, two, three, four—then blow the trapped air out of my lungs, willing my rapid breathing to slow down.

I scold myself for not calling ahead. But then I counter if I had called, Emma might have ignored me, or worse—told me not to come at all.

It's the middle of the day. The apartments appear deserted. Most of the residents are probably at work. As far as I know, Emma doesn't have a job yet, but she could be running errands. I really should have put more thought into this and not assumed she would be home. Maybe it's best if she's not. I could forget about this whole thing and head home. I'm not surprised by how much the last idea appeals to me.

I climb the concrete steps to the fourth floor where Emma and Philip's apartment is located. Walking up the steps is somewhat beneficial, momentarily pushing the blood from my overthinking brain to my legs. Huffing, I stand in front of apartment 409, trying to catch my breath. I know it's the right apartment because of the colorful sunflower doormat with the words "Welcome to the Polks." Staring down at it, I smile at the cuteness, but then the mother alarm blares in my head. Why would she put their last name outside the door where anyone sketchy could find them? I bend to flip the mat over and hide their name. "What am I doing?" I mutter under my breath and stop myself.

Straightening my back, I reach out and rap on the door. *Tap, tap, tap.* I wait with bated breath, but neither Emma nor Philip answers. I press my ear to the door, listening for a radio, TV, or any sign of activity inside. Nothing. I let out a sigh of relief, not knowing what I was going to say or do if Emma did answer. But to be this close and not see her replaces the relief from a moment ago with crushing disappointment.

My mind wanders to when Emma was younger. Her small soft arms hugging my neck while sprinkling wet kisses across my cheeks. Reading bedtime stories snuggled together in my grandma's old rocking chair. Hosting slumber parties for her and her friends. Her shy wave from the stage of an elementary school program. Late-night talks after high school soccer games. An all-day dress shopping spree for the next big dance. How did Emma and I go from "besties," as she liked to call us, to hardly speaking at all?

"Mom?" Emma's voice calls from behind me.

I whip around, almost losing my balance.

She stands an arm's length away, dressed in an oversized gray T-shirt—probably Phillip's—a black pair of leggings, and flip-flops. Her shoulder-length black hair is in its usual messy bun.

My eyes mist at the sight of her. It feels like a lifetime has passed since I've seen her face-to-face, even though it's only been a few weeks. Her arms hug a laundry basket filled with folded clothes and towels. She drops it at her feet, closes the distance between us, and wraps her arms around me. My heart overflows with the realization she's happy to see me.

"Is Dad here too?" Her voice is hopeful as she releases me.

"No, just me." I don't explain more.

Worry lines cross her brow. "Is everything okay?"

"Yes, we're both fine," I assure her. "Your dad didn't know I was coming here." I grimace. "I didn't know I was coming here."

Her eyes grow wide, and she tilts her head. "What? You, the person who plans everything to the minutest detail? Where does he think you are?"

A man and woman stare at us as they pass by on the corridor. Ducking my head closer to Emma, I ask. "Can we go inside?"

"Of course." She puts her key in the lock and swings the door wide open. I reach for the laundry basket, but Emma says, "I've got it," and picks it up from the concrete entryway.

I follow her inside and shut the door behind me. She disappears into another room for a beat, then returns without the basket. Not wanting to intrude on her and Philip's privacy, I stay at my spot by the door.

"Would you like a tour?" Emma smiles, but her eyebrows furrow.

"I would love that." I'm thankful for any delay in answering her questions.

"The apartment's small and we could use a little more furniture, but we like it," she says, pride beaming from her face.

Even though their apartment is filled with secondhand store finds, she's made it cozy. Handmade doilies cover the weathered arms of a brown-and-tan plaid couch. The kitchen table has a beautiful hand-embroidered sunflower table runner, which distracts from the scratches and heat impressions left by the previous owner's lack of care. A faint scent of fresh paint rises from the four white chairs surrounding the oak table. Pride fills my heart at how Emma has made their apartment a home.

I smile, remembering the first home Dave and I shared. It was also a one-bedroom apartment. Dave had started his first grown-up job after graduating. I was working at the university bookstore. We were poor but felt rich. We ate a lot of ramen noodles. Rent, food, and utilities used up most of our money. But if we had any cash left at the end of the month, we stashed it away, hoping to save enough for my next semester's tuition.

With one positive pregnancy test, my college career moved to the back burner. Our small savings went to buy a baby bed, formula, diapers, and other necessities. But Emma was the blessing I didn't know I needed. All thoughts of college disappeared. Being a full-time mom was enough for me.

With the tour of her apartment finished, we take a seat on the couch. The moment of truth arrives when Emma asks, "Now, Mother, why are you here? And why doesn't Dad know you're here?"

Chest pounding, I reply, "You're not going to like it."

Her body stiffens.

My palms begin to sweat. After taking a deep breath in and exhaling it, I say, "I was crushed the day you dropped the news of your elopement, so I ran away."

Emma snickers, but when I don't laugh, her smile fades. "Mom, really?" Her tone turns harsh. "This is about me getting married? I know you were disappointed I didn't have the formal wedding ceremony *you* planned, but isn't running away from home a little dramatic?"

My lungs constrict. I can't draw enough air to speak. Tears

build behind my eyes, but I'm determined to hold them off. No more crying. It's time I get real with my daughter. "It was never about the ceremony. That's not what disappointed me. I was looking forward to spending more time with you," I explain. "We've grown so distant since you headed off to college. I had hoped planning your wedding would bring us closer, like we used to be."

Emma opens her mouth, but I raise my index finger. Her lips purse. A muscle in her jaw twitches, but she waits.

"You excluded me from one of the most important days of your life," I choke out. "Do you know how much that hurt?"

She lowers her gaze. Whatever she was going to say, she won't express it now. With a heavy sigh, Emma gives me a pained expression. "I'm sorry."

I open my mouth, but no words come out. Swallowing hard, I nod.

"And what about Dad?" Her voice trembles as she searches my face.

Seeing the fear flash across her eyes, I assure her again. "He's fine. We're fine. I got a little upset when I found out he knew about the elopement and didn't tell me. Sounds like everyone knew but me." I grimace. Then, locking eyes with Emma, I say, "He told me I needed to get a life. A life that didn't center around you."

Emma gasps, then covers her mouth with her palm.

"I know. 'Way harsh,' huh?" I quote a funny line from one of Emma's favorite movies.

She blinks at me. Neither of us laughs.

"Anyway, I ran away on a whim, hoping to figure out how to get a life, and ended up on your doorstep. Back to square one."

She takes my hands. "Well, I'm glad you're here." Her big brown eyes glisten. "I am sorry," she says again.

A lump forms in my throat. The pained expression in her eyes lets me know she's sincere.

"You're right. I regret not having Dad and you at the courthouse. It was bittersweet."

I squeeze her hands, giving her a wistful smile.

Emotionally spent, I'm grateful when Emma changes the subject. "How many days do you plan on staying?" She checks the calendar on the kitchen wall. I'm sure she has plans that don't include me crashing in unexpectedly.

"Only the afternoon," I say.

"Oh, okay." She lets out a breath, then blushes. "You're welcome to stay longer. We would just need to reschedule a few things."

"It's okay. I'm ready to go home." I give her a reassuring smile. "But before I go, can we order some pizza? I'm starving," I say. "We can catch up while we wait for it to be delivered. Like we used to."

Emma orders our usual hand-tossed pepperoni and mushroom from a nearby pizza place, then shifts her focus back to me. We sit cross-legged on her couch, facing each other like we often did at home. Emma tells me all about Philip's new job, a restaurant they tried out, and a list of places they want to visit in the city.

Without warning, she jumps in her seat, squealing. "Guess what?" Before I can respond, she says, "I wanted to tell you and Dad at the same time, but I can't hold it in any longer." Her eyes gleam with excitement and her smile lights up the room. "I enrolled at Arizona State University for the fall semester. They took almost all my credits. I talked to a college advisor there, and she said I should be able to finish my degree by next summer."

"That's wonderful, Emma." I clap. "I'm so happy for you." I know my smile doesn't reach my eyes. A part of me rejoices in knowing she's going to finish her college degree, but the mom in me grieves listening to her talk about the life she and Philip have planned together. One that doesn't include me. The reality she's no longer "my" little girl is a hard pill to swallow.

She tilts her head to stare at me, then asks in a soft voice, "What's wrong?"

My facial expressions must've given me away again. I should've concealed the conflict inside me better.

"Can you make a little space for me?" My voice cracks.

She sits quiet for a moment, a puzzled expression on her face.

"You don't need me anymore," I whisper. "Is this where our story ends—you and me?"

"Of course not, Mom. I'll always need you, but not like I did when I was little. This isn't the end. It's the same book, but a different chapter. And who knows—this one might be better than the last," she says.

With tears in my eyes, I say, "But nothing compares to raising you."

"Well, maybe not." She chuckles. "I am pretty awesome." When she hugs me, a tear runs down her right cheek onto mine.

She releases me and places her hand on her heart. "You'll always have a place in my life and a special place in my heart. You're my mom."

Not wanting Emma to see the pain in my eyes, I lower my gaze to my hands folded in my lap. "I miss you. I'm having a hard time recalibrating. You are all the chapters in my book, all the eggs in my basket, the whole kit and caboodle."

Emma laughs. I raise my eyes, chuckling too, knowing how ridiculous I sound.

She purses her lips again, then lifts them into a mischievous smile. "I'm sorry, Mom, but you did this to yourself. You raised me to be a strong and independent woman, so you get what you get."

"I suppose." I shrug.

A loud knock on the door startles us.

"Pizza delivery," a man yells from outside.

I hand Emma some money, but she tosses it back.

"It's already paid for." She points at her phone. "I used the app." Grinning, she jogs to the door.

After eating two slices, I check my watch. I need to go if I'm going to catch my flight. Maybe I should have booked it for tomorrow. My throat constricts at the melancholy atmosphere between us. Leaving her always feels wrong, but I know in my heart that it's time to go. Goodbyes are hard.

After a long hug, I shut the door behind me. Standing in the empty corridor, I ponder Emma's words.

"I'll always need you, Mom." Words I needed to hear.

The hazy dark cloud that's filled my thoughts gives way to mental clarity. I'm tired of treading water, stuck in one place and bobbing for air. If I don't let go of the picture-perfect life in my head, I'll drown. And I want to swim.

# CHAPTER THIRTY-FIVE

The sunshine streaming through the windshield reflects off the red slipper charm on my bracelet. A kaleidoscope of light cascades across the dash. If only I could click my heels three times and be home.

The Phoenix Sky Harbor International Airport is not far from Emma's apartment. A big sign to the right of the highway shows me the way to the entrance. Humming happily, I turn toward the sign that reads Rental Car Center. I'm quick to park, grab my luggage from the back, and hand over the key to an attendant. I smile as he jumps in the SUV and drives off with Delores's and my getaway car. Before I allow nostalgia to run away with me, I walk through the double glass door. With a new spring in my step, I stride toward my terminal. I can't wait to go home.

My phone dings several times while I'm checking in at the ticket counter. The airline agent scowls at me, so I ignore the texts. Once my luggage is checked and I have my ticket in hand, I search for a seat. My flight won't board for another hour.

Rows of attached yellow metal chairs fill the small terminal waiting area. Plopping down in one of the seats, I grab my cell out of my purse. Three missed messages. One from Delores, one from Bea, and one from Agnus. All of them wish me safe travels home. At the end of Delores's text, she reminds me I'm expected at Irene's on Thursday for salsa lessons.

Chuckling, I text back.

I'll be there.

Still holding the phone in my hand, I jump when it rings. My pulse quickens when Dave's mom's name pops up on the screen.

"Peggy?" My mother-in-law rarely calls unless she can't reach Dave. "Is everything okay?"

"Yes, yes. We're okay," Peggy assures me in her Texan drawl. "I just wanted to check on you."

I squeeze my eyes shut, wondering what Dave has told her. I try to sound relaxed, but my voice is strained when I say, "I'm good."

She gives an audible sigh, then a gap of silence follows. I cross and uncross my legs, waiting for her to say more.

Peggy clears her throat, breaking the silence. "Do you have a minute to talk?"

My stomach sinks, dreading another confrontation. "Of course." I glance at my watch, secretly hoping it's time to board.

"Dave tells me you've been on quite the adventure."

My face grows hot. I pull at the collar of my white button-down blouse. "Yes, but it's over now. I'm at the airport. I'll be flying home soon." I'm irritated Dave outed me to his mother.

Peggy gives what sounds to be a sigh of relief followed by, "Oh, Sarah, that makes my heart so happy."

My mouth falls open, and my eyes grow wide. I'm surprised she's not mad I took off and left her son. My voice shakes. "Peggy, I'm sorry I worried you. I shouldn't have left like I did."

"Don't apologize. You don't have to explain anything to me. You don't think I never took off once in a while to blow off steam or have a thought my kids or husband didn't interrupt? I had five kids, for gracious sake." She chuckles.

Picturing Peggy running off, taking a break from her family, doesn't match up with the image I've created. She always seemed the example of a perfect mother.

"You did?" I ask, incredulous.

She laughs harder. "I'm not proud of those moments, but it was the only way to keep my sanity. Anyway, Dave has been calling me daily, all in a fizz. He told me about your argument, about Emma eloping, and the last thing he said to you before you left. Yikes."

Shaking my head, I try to rein in my spinning thoughts. Pulling at my collar again, I wonder what else he shared.

As if reading my mind, Peggy says, "I was surprised he told me anything. He's so private. He never shares anything about you, him, or Emma—other than the usual surface stuff. You know, Emma's school events, et cetera."

A sigh of relief escapes my lips.

"Because Dave is so private"—Peggy pauses, seeming to carefully weigh each word—"I've never asked, even though I wondered."

When she continues to hesitate, I ask, "Wondered what?"

"How you're doing. Really. You don't know how many times throughout the years I've wanted to ask you that—all the way back to your wedding day."

"Really?" I'm taken aback by her admission.

"Yes. I sometimes think about your wedding. Your dad had just passed. Dave and you hadn't known each other long before you married. Then you got pregnant with Emma. That's a lot in a short amount of time. How did you handle it all at such a young age?"

My forehead wrinkles, and my mind races, remembering. I never considered all that was going on until now. I answer her with two words. "Your son."

There's a brief pause, then a few sniffles from Peggy's end before she speaks again. "Hank and I were worried when Dave called to tell us he'd met *the one*. A few months later, he called to invite us to your wedding. I'll be honest, Sarah. We were upset and worried he was making a terrible mistake. We hadn't even met you." Peggy's voice rises.

While Emma's elopement was a surprise, at least we knew Philip. I never doubted their love for each other.

Remorseful for never thinking about how Dave's parents must have felt until now, I say, "I'm so sorry we put you through that. I can't imagine Emma marrying someone we never met."

Peggy sniffles again before she says, "But then you stepped through the church entryway, a tiny young woman covered in white lace. I watched as you walked down the aisle alone to my son. I'd never seen him so happy. It's a wonder the buttons on his shirt didn't pop off with how his chest puffed out with pride. The smile on his face was so bright, it could have lit New York City. His eyes never left your face. It wasn't until you returned his gaze that all our doubts disappeared."

Grateful tears fill my eyes. "I loved him so much then, and even more now. I hope you know that," I say with fervor, praying she believes me.

"I do, and I told him that too. I also told him this trip isn't about him. Men always think everything is about them." She chuckles softly.

A couple engrossed in conversation a few feet away remind me I'm not alone. I swipe a tear from my eye before it rolls down my cheek.

"Before we hang up, please let me tell you one more thing," Peggy says.

"Okaaay." There's more?

"I regret never telling you what a wonderful mother you've been to our granddaughter."

Closing my eyes, I tip my head back for a moment. Like a healing balm to my heart, her words sooth the scars of doubt planted the moment I laid eyes on my tiny brown-eyed baby.

Placing a hand on my chest, I try to compose myself. My voice full of emotion, I say in a low tone, "Thank you, Peggy. You don't know how much that means to me." Heavy, happy tears fill my eyes and stream down my face. There's no stopping them now. "Being a mom is hard." My voice cracks. "I never knew if I was doing it right. I only knew I loved her so much."

Peggy clears her throat. "I'm not sure what transpired between you two, but she's thankful for you. She told me so."

I swallow hard, my throat thick with emotion.

"I'm sorry I didn't reach out to you sooner," she says. "You always seemed so put together. I didn't want to intrude."

Me? Together? Funny how people perceive others, not knowing who they really are inside. I guess I've been guilty of this too.

"Oh, I'm also sorry my boneheaded son was so insensitive," she adds. "Takes after his dad, I'm afraid. Do you know I cried every time one of our kids left home and I had to set one less plate on the dinner table? Henry would say, 'It'll be fine.'

Basically, 'walk it off.' Eventually it got better, but in that moment, I thought the sadness would never go away."

"Flight number 220 for Springfield, Missouri, now boarding," blares from the airport speakers.

"I'm sorry, but I have to go," I tell Peggy. "My flight is boarding." Still connected to her, I grab my suitcase with one hand and hold the cell to my ear with the other hand.

"Of course. I'm sorry I talked so long. Just know I'm only a phone call away if you ever need to talk," Peggy says.

Pleased and overwhelmed by her kindness, I say, "Thank you."

The phone clicks, ending the call. My cell goes back to the screensaver of Emma. I smile at her image before shoving my phone into my purse. People are lining up at the terminal gate.

Pulling my carry-on behind me, I join the group of passengers. Walking into the plane's cabin, I'm a little disappointed a large group of women isn't there to cheer me on. I scrunch through the small aisle with my carry-on, searching for my assigned seat. The plane is only at half capacity. The window seat beside me is vacant, so I move into it and tuck myself away. As I glance from the view outside to the front of the cabin, a flight attendant gives us the safety demonstration. I miss Bob—and his clipboard.

Closing my eyes, I drift in the space between wakefulness and sleep. My thoughts land on last night's phone conversation with Dave.

"I'm coming home." I pray he's happy with my announcement.

He doesn't respond. My mouth goes dry at the silence on the other end of the line. My stomach knots as I wait.

Then there's a sob. When he finally speaks, his voice cracks. "Good."

I don't want to embarrass him, but I have to know. "Are you crying?"

"Maybe," he answers timidly.

I can only remember two times when Dave cried—*ever*. Once when we said our wedding vows, and again the first time he held Emma. My heart goes out to him. I wish I could wrap my arms around his waist to comfort him and erase the pain I've caused.

"I was so scared I lost you," he says sadly.

"Never," I exclaim. "I lost my way for a while." I pause. "But you will never lose me," I proclaim with all the love and tenderness my heart holds.

Dave's voice trembles. "I'm so sorry for what I said, Sarah."

"It was a little harsh, but I needed to hear it," I say. "I was stuck in my wallowing."

He blows out a loud sigh of relief before he speaks. "Oh, Sarah, you sound good." His gruff baritone returns, and my stomach flutters. "I can't wait for you to get home. I've missed you."

I've missed him too. We've been at odds for so long, I don't want to waste any more time with him being sad.

"Dave, do you remember how you proposed?" I ask in a flirtatious tone.

He laughs. "Yeah, it wasn't the most romantic proposal."

"It was to me." Nostalgia takes over. "Dad had rented a house close to campus to live in while I finished school, but then he passed away my junior year. We had only been dating a few months. I didn't have the means to pay the rent. I was on the phone, trying to find a studio apartment to move into, when you walked in. My eyes were red and swollen from crying, and snot was running down my face. I was in a pair of old jeans and one of my dad's sweatshirts. I don't think I'd even combed my hair. I'm sure I looked a mess."

"That's not the way I remember it," Dave says. "I knocked on the door, but you didn't answer. So I checked the knob. It was unlocked. I walked into your living room and found you sitting on the floor surrounded by a pile of half-packed boxes, one ear to the phone, motioning me inside. I thought to myself, *She's the most beautiful girl I've ever seen, and I want her to be mine —always.*"

"Love is blind." I chuckle, but those butterflies in my stomach are back.

Dave continues, "I sat down beside you, looked into your beautiful green eyes, and asked you to marry me."

"Why then? Why that moment?" I ask, confused why he would tie himself to someone who had so many sad things going on.

"I wanted to be there for you, in the good and the bad times. You weren't a mess. You were grieving. I wanted to help you through the loss of your dad. But I have to admit, I also knew your grief would fade. Then you'd realize you were stronger than you gave yourself credit for. Selfishly, I didn't want any other guy to have the privilege of loving you when that happened. Don't you realize how wonderful you are? If only you could see yourself through my eyes."

My face warms. My heart is overwhelmed with the love I carry for this man.

We married two weeks after my dad's funeral in a tiny chapel off campus. A minister we didn't know presided over our vows. No friends or family were in attendance, except Dave's parents who flew up from Texas. I walked myself down the aisle with a bouquet of wildflowers I picked on the way to the church. Dave wore the navy-blue interview suit his parents helped him buy earlier that year. His right pants pocket held the two simple gold bands we purchased the week before from a local pawn store.

Hoping someday Dave would propose, I had visited a small bridal boutique a few blocks from campus. Displayed in the window was a white lace-and-taffeta wedding dress with quarter-length sleeves and a long train. On a whim, I tried it on. The puffy sleeves adorned with white satin ribbons and the fitted bodice reminded me of the wedding dress Princess Diana wore when she married Prince Charles. The dress fit perfectly.

After paying for my dad's funeral from his savings, I barely had enough money left for the gown. It was frivolous. Dave had just graduated and hadn't earned his first paycheck at his new job. What little he had saved, he put down as a deposit and the first month's rent for the studio apartment we would live in once we were married.

I could have bought a simple dress that cost much less so we could use the extra money for necessary things—like food. But all doubt disappeared the moment Dave saw me walking toward him in that church. His dazzling smile—the pride beaming from his face—gave me peace about my decision. I wanted to be beautiful for him.

I wish my dad could've been there. His loss left a terrible void in my life. A lot of tearful nights followed his death. But two months after our wedding, I got the news we were expecting a baby. My sorrow turned to joy.

"What do you think about planning a trip when I get home?"

"I'm not sure Emma and Philip can go right now with his new job," he says.

"I wasn't planning on asking Emma and Philip," I say in a coy tone.

"Really?" Surprise fills his voice.

"Dave Goodwin, you owe me a honeymoon. I've waited long enough."

My heartbeat quickens at his low masculine chuckle on the other end. "I think that's doable." He's flirting with me.

"But we need to take our vacation before my digital photography class begins at the community college," I say sheepishly.

"I love that idea, Sarah," Dave says. "About time you get back to it. You always had a great eye. I'm sure the local newspaper would love a freelance photographer."

"Well, I was thinking of going a different direction. Maybe start a small home-photography studio when I'm ready. I could practice with our neighbors, Olivia and her kids. Offer her some free family portraits, if she's game." Another idea pings before Dave can comment. "Oh, we could make some small wooden structures in our backyard for photo backgrounds and maybe some props too?" My voice rises with enthusiasm. "Also, what do you think about me transforming Emma's bedroom—"

"Yes." He gives an emphatic yell.

"Wait, you didn't let me finish." I giggle. I'm probably overwhelming him.

"Oh, sorry," he says. "It's nice to hear enthusiasm in your voice again. I've missed it."

I pause. The sense of purpose rising in me feels good. My creative juices flowing, I say, "I want to transform Emma's bedroom into an office. I wonder if Olivia would like a four-poster princess bed for her daughter? Maybe I'll have them over for dinner when I get back. If it's okay with Olivia, Mia can go through Emma's toys and take home her favorites. Did you know Mia loves mermaids just like Emma did when she was that age?"

"It all sounds great, Sarah." I wonder if it's possible to hear a smile.

My cell chimes, bringing me back to the present. A few passengers are still boarding, so I answer my phone.

"I'll be waiting for you at the airport. I'll be the guy with the big goofy smile on his face," Dave teases.

"Sounds great." I grin.

I hear the cabin door lock. The stewardess at the front points to me, then motions to turn off my cell. "I have to go, Dave. We're getting ready to take off. I'll see you soon."

"I can't wait," he says.

I touch my fingers to my lips, excited for the adventures to come. *Neither can I.*

# ACKNOWLEDGMENTS

Thank you, Mr. Robert Rose, my high school English teacher. You acted like everything I wrote was amazing. Looking back at some of those early writings, you should have won an Oscar. Thanks for believing in me.

Thank you to my wonderful nephew, Nick York. Even though I had a little fun with the fictional sheriff's department in my story, you helped me navigate the proper police protocol used in various scenarios. I learned a lot. You are a credit to your police department.

Thank you to my pastor and friend, Larry Dugger. You introduced me to my first writers' conference, helping me connect to agents and publishers. I was extremely nervous to attend, but your encouragement along the way helped me stay the course.

Thank you to my Beta Readers—Rhea Anne Matthews and Barbara Smith. Handing off my rough draft was hard. Being vulnerable is not an easy task. Thank you for your kind words, suggestions, and encouragement. I'm blessed to call you friends.

Thank you to all my friends and family who have encouraged my writing journey.

Thank you Scrivening Press editors—Suzie Waltner and Denica McCall. I appreciate the time and dedication you took to make my story better.

Last, but certainly not least, thank you Linda Fulkerson for taking a chance on me. I'll forever be grateful to you and Scrivenings Press for making a life-long dream a reality. There are no adequate words to describe my gratitude for all you've done for me.

# ABOUT THE AUTHOR

Janell Goodrich York lives in the Ozarks with her husband. Finding her third act has been a challenge, but beach trips with her husband, writing, and spoiling her grandkids and two puppies have helped the process. This is her first novel.

# RECENT TITLES FROM SCRIVENINGS PRESS

Tavo Morales has returned to Valiant, Texas, to stir the embers of a relationship with the woman he has never stopped loving, but hidden reefs from his past threaten to destroy his future.

Paige Muñoz wants her new event planning business to be a success and won't let anything stand in her way. But the path she's on to make her dreams come true proves dangerous.

Is the love Tavo and Paige once shared strong enough to survive his secrets and her stubbornness?

Get your copy here:

https://scrivenings.link/waitinonpaige

\* \* \*

Ella dreams of her artwork on display in the famous Prince Gallery, but working for her stepmother leaves her eking out sporadic minutes to draw or paint. When her stepsister steals her drawing and claims it as her own, Ella fears she's lost her chance.

Chaz Prince wants more responsibility at his family's gallery, but first he must prove he can handle it. Chaz talks his dad into a contest to bring in some new artists, sure this will be exactly what the gallery needs. When he stumbles across Ella's piece, he not only wants the artwork, but wishes to know the artist too.

At the gala to celebrate the contest winners, Ella is determined to let them know the artwork is hers, but time is against her. And where did her shoe end up?

\* \* \*

*Stay up-to-date on your favorite books and authors with our free e-newsletters.*

ScriveningsPress.com